"It seems to me that you've just acquired a new lover."

Adam caressed her cheek, his eyes teasing. "Is it bedtime yet? I've decided my patience is running out."

She stirred uneasily beneath his laughing gaze. "Oh, come on, Adam, don't be crazy. You know pretending to be my lover wouldn't work. Anybody looking at us would see that we're just good friends."

"Pretend that you're in love with me. Would that be such a difficult thing to do?"

Her hands twisted into a knot. "It isn't only me who would have to pretend."

"I think you're underestimating my acting ability. If you like, I'll prove—"

"That isn't necessary, Adam. You know the idea would never—"

Before she could say anything further, she felt his lips move caressingly against her throat, then he captured her mouth in a hard, angry kiss...

Jasmine Craig *was born in Wales, worked in the British Foreign Office in Rio de Janeiro, Brazil, and is now married and the mother of four children. Her family has lived in nine places around the world in the last sixteen years. She started writing because it was a career she could pursue anywhere.*

Dear Reader:

If the New Year always catches you by surprise, as it does me, you'll especially appreciate this month's SECOND CHANCE AT LOVE romances, which are sure to make the adjustment to 1985 fun and easy. Read on to learn a little bit about each one; in fact, from now on in this space I'll be revealing intriguing tidbits about the current month's books and their authors. Hints about next month's books will still appear on the inside back cover, and we've also added a two-page questionnaire, which I hope you'll fill out. The information you provide will keep us in touch with exactly what kinds of books you most enjoy.

First on the January list is *Knight of Passion* (#238) by Linda Barlow. Judging from the responses we've received, Linda has quickly become one of your favorite writers. In this whimsical, poignant romance, Philippa and Jeff—a pair as modern as they come—begin to suspect they were doomed lovers in another life centuries ago. After all those eons, the two combatants are still literally crossing swords. Talk about long arguments! Also, keep a sharp eye out for Bret and Daniel from Linda's *Bewitched* (#224), who make cameo appearances here.

Frances Davies, another favorite writer, will knock your socks off with *Mysterious East* (#239). A frivolous disguise plunges Karen East into the world's zaniest identity crisis with golden Viking Erik Søndersen, and deceptions pile onto deceptions faster than you can say "Sherlock Holmes." Prepare yourself for the most unusual seduction . . . by artichoke! *Mysterious East* is a thoroughly delectable romp.

Bed of Roses (#240) is by new author Jean Fauré, a gifted dreamweaver who writes with heart-wrenching impact. She also knows the ins and outs of roses—she has a greenhouse in her own back yard. I think you'll find *Bed of Roses* refreshingly different and emotionally involving.

Bridge of Dreams (#241) is another enchanting romance from Helen Carter, author of *Touched by Lightning* (#194), which so many of you praised in your letters. Helen's characters really tug at your heartstrings, and her stories have a way of gently captivating you until you can't put them down. In this book, Liz Forsyth and Josh Gates's urgent involvement proves Helen's powers of seduction once again.

Jean Barrett—another new "Jean" for SECOND CHANCE AT LOVE—has written a breathtakingly sensual and compelling story. *Fire Bird* (#242) begins with a dramatic plane crash on a remote, ice-bound island and continues with three days of all-consuming passion between Carly and "Skyhawk." A touch of mystery and Skyhawk's imminent departure make this romance particularly effective.

Finally, in *Dear Adam* (#243) Jasmine Craig creates two memorable males—Damion Tanner, whom Lynn Frampton *thinks* she loves, and Adam Hunter, whom you'll *know* she loves. Once again, Jasmine creates strong sexual tension with skillful subtlety. And don't feel too bad about Damion—you just may see more of him later!

Be sure to treat yourself well this January by escaping the holiday confusion and relaxing with all six SECOND CHANCE AT LOVE romances. Before you know it, you'll be writing 1985 instead of 1984 on your correspondence, and you'll realize you've adjusted to a new beginning after all!

Warm wishes for a Happy New Year!

Ellen Edwards

Ellen Edwards, Senior Editor
SECOND CHANCE AT LOVE
The Berkley Publishing Group
200 Madison Avenue
New York, N.Y. 10016

Second Chance at Love®

DEAR ADAM

JASMINE CRAIG

A
SECOND CHANCE AT LOVE
BOOK

Second Chance at Love books are published by
The Berkley Publishing Group
200 Madison Avenue, New York, NY 10016

CHAPTER ONE

WHEN LYNN FRAMPTON walked into the darkened rehearsal room, Damion Tanner was preparing to murder his mistress. Lynn watched as he paced the makeshift stage, noticing how he dominated the action by the sheer force of his presence. He reached out and touched Christine, his leading lady, on the cheek. Slowly, sensuously, he brushed his fingers along the line of her jaw, until they came to rest on her parted lips. By a subtle movement of his body he managed to convey that the tender gesture concealed hatred rather than affection.

Lynn watched in silent admiration as the scene moved to its inevitable climax. She had read the script and knew exactly what would happen, but she had been too busy to watch any previous rehearsals, and she found that she was holding her breath as Damion

1

reached into his pocket and withdrew the switchblade that would kill the woman he loved.

Lynn's hands convulsively gripped the manuscript she was holding. Damion's knuckles gleamed white around the slender handle of the knife, then he flung himself on top of his mistress, the slump of his shoulders portraying an agonized mixture of love, bitterness, and pathological anger. Christine's scream rang out sharp and piercing in the darkness before ending in a brief, sickening gurgle.

For a few moments there was total silence in the rehearsal room, then a ripple of applause rose, followed by a rush of compliments from the director. The supposed murder victim sprang to her feet, smiling triumphantly, her long hair gleaming with an enticing silver shimmer under the brilliant glow of the arc lights.

Lynn exhaled in a slow sigh. For a split second she had been so caught up in the power of Damion's acting that she had almost expected to see blood gushing from Christine's throat, even though the set still boasted no scenery and only minimal props.

The arc lights were switched off, and the main lights came up in the auditorium. Lynn found a chair and waited patiently while the director assembled the cast on stage and made some general observations about the rehearsal.

Damion looked tired, but he listened carefully to the director's comments. His leading lady was less attentive. She nestled against his side, splaying her fingers possessively around his rib cage and nuzzling his cheek. He draped an arm around her shoulders but, to Lynn's searching gaze, it seemed clear that he wasn't giving any particular thought to his actions. Wherever his mind was, it certainly didn't seem to be on Christine.

Lynn closed her eyes, warning herself not to see signs of boredom that weren't really there. She had worked for Damion for ten months now, during which time she had watched him conduct love affairs with no less than three of his leading ladies. Christine Mitchell was his most recent mistress, and until today, their affair had seemed to blaze with white-hot intensity.

Looking at Damion again, Lynn had no doubt about the tedium etched onto his handsome features. Her heart gave a small leap of hope, and then she frowned, angry at her own foolishness. Just because Damion was losing interest in Christine didn't mean he was ready to notice that Lynn was a living, breathing woman with all the normal female attributes in all the right places. His television series had recently acquired a new leading lady, Tiffany Brandon, an exotic dark-haired creature with enormous breasts and a minuscule intellect. If Damion ran true to form, he was far more likely to fall in love with Tiffany than with Lynn, his office manager, whom he had yet to notice was anything more than an efficient piece of office furniture.

The director dismissed the cast, and Damion glanced out into the small auditorium, waving cheerfully as soon as he spotted Lynn. He jumped off the low stage and walked quickly toward her.

"Hello, babe," he said, ruffling her short brown curls in a casual greeting. "How's things at the office?"

"Busy. Worse than most Fridays. Your tax accountant's frantic about last month's expense report; your agent called seven times; your publicity consultant wants you to attend the premiere of a new movie; my secretary's buried under your latest pile of fan mail. But everything's under control."

He clapped her on the shoulder. "That's what I like

to hear! Damn, you're a fabulous manager, Lynn! I don't know how I coped before I found you."

She felt herself blush. "You're a talented actor, Damion, and I like taking some of the routine hassles out of your life. If I organize your office efficiently, you're left free to concentrate on your acting."

"I'm delighted you feel that way, honey. I hope you never decide to quit, because I don't think I could survive without you." His mouth crinkled into its famous heart-stopping grin, and his eyes darkened to a devastating shade of midnight blue. At that moment he looked about five times sexier than his publicity photos, which was an almost unbelievable achievement.

Somehow Lynn managed to return his smile, wondering for the thousandth time how she contrived to look so cheerful when her heart was undoubtedly breaking. Maybe those years of acting class hadn't been wasted after all.

"Did you come downtown to watch me rehearse?" Damion asked. "Everything went pretty well, I thought. I've been coaching Christine for two weeks, and she's finally gotten that last scene right."

"Yes, everything looked good. You were outstanding, Damion. But I didn't come just to watch the rehearsal. I came to bring you this movie script. I...uh...I wasn't sure if you'd be going back to your own apartment tonight, and your agent's anxious to hear your opinion. He had the script flown in from Los Angeles this afternoon, and he'd like to have your reaction as soon as possible. I've already glanced through it, and I think you should read it right away. Your agent's right—it's absolute dynamite, and it's a red-hot property."

"I'll give it a shot tomorrow, but hell, Lynn, I'm tired. This crazy schedule's beginning to get to me."

He yawned, stretching languorously.

"I can believe it," she said, thinking despairingly that even his yawn was sexy. It wasn't fair that one man could wrap up so much eroticism and so much acting talent in a single seductive package. No wonder he had already won two Emmys and a Golden Globe Award. And no wonder that the ratings for his television series hovered permanently in the stratosphere. He practically burned up the airwaves that transmitted his program.

She watched silently as he flicked through the first few pages of the script. After a couple of minutes he snapped it shut, rubbing his hand briefly across his eyes.

"Tough day?" she inquired sympathetically.

"No worse than usual, I guess. Hell, I'll be glad when this season's taping is over. Sometimes I think that rehearsing a Broadway play *and* doing a television series is too much even for me."

"You should get more rest, Damion. You've been working too hard."

"I know, but what can I do about it? I'm in demand, babe. Everybody wants me."

"Especially me." Christine Mitchell's voice broke into their conversation, her eyes smoldering with sensual promise as she curled herself into Damion's arms. "Isn't it time for us to leave, darling? You've been talking to Lynn for *hours*, and you promised to take me to that new nightclub."

"Did I? I'd forgotten, but I guess we may as well go. I'm too strung out to sleep and too tired to read."

Christine trailed her fingers inside the open neck of his shirt, and Damion's air of mingled boredom and fatigue faded, although it didn't entirely disappear.

"Let's get out of here," Christine said huskily, leaning her head on his shoulder.

"Okay." He yawned again. "I'll come in a minute. Don't rush me." He lifted her hand and kissed the tips of her fingers absentmindedly.

Lynn swallowed hard and stared determinedly toward the deserted stage. It was, she decided suddenly, past time for her to go home.

"Have a good night, you two," she said, turning abruptly toward the nearest exit. "I'll see you on Monday, Damion."

"Wait a minute, sugar. I've been thinking about that new script. I'd like you to stop by my apartment tomorrow so we can go over it together. I need your input, Lynn. You have a real talent for visualizing how the bare bones of a script will look when it's actually up on the screen."

She flushed with pleasure at his compliment. She'd planned to leave early in the morning to visit her parents in Connecticut, but it was flattering to know that Damion needed her advice on such an important matter. With a little juggling she could rearrange her schedule. Her parents weren't planning anything special, so her exact time of arrival didn't much matter. She could catch a later train and still be with her family by dinnertime.

"It will have to be in the morning, Damion," she said. "I'm going to visit my parents in the afternoon."

He looked put out. "You know I'm not at my best in the morning, Lynn. Can't you change your plans?"

"I guess I could, but you have a meeting with the editor from *People* magazine tomorrow at three. There wouldn't be much time for us to discuss the script if I came by in the afternoon."

"Oh, well, in that case I suppose the morning will have to do. I'll see you around ten o'clock, Lynn."

"Not a moment before," Christine interjected, her voice distinctly sulky.

"No, of course not. I'll be there at ten sharp."

"Thanks, babe." Damion acknowledged her words with another dazzling smile, then he walked toward the exit, Christine clinging to his waist. "See you tomorrow, Lynn," he called, not looking back.

Lynn stood for a few minutes staring silently at the closed door, then with a weary shrug of her shoulders, she turned and headed toward the side exit. It had been a long week, she realized, and she was exhausted.

It was almost nine o'clock by the time she arrived back at her own small apartment in the east eighties. She kicked off her shoes next to the front door, luxuriating in the welcome sense of homecoming, wriggling her toes in the soft, beige carpet as she crossed the living room to her tiny kitchen. Manhattan rents were outrageous and absurd compared to anywhere else in the country, and not many single women could afford the pleasure of living alone. The generous salary Damion paid her was just one more reason to feel grateful to him. He had given her two hefty raises in the ten months she had worked for him. It was good to know that he appreciated the organization she had brought into his previously chaotic life.

She opened the refrigerator door and examined the sparsely stocked shelves with a faint feeling of irritation. Half a loaf of sliced wheat bread, a stick of margarine, a carton of plain yogurt, and three eggs. Too busy to go out for lunch, she had asked her secretary to bring back some yogurt and frozen fruit juice. She didn't want to eat the same thing again tonight, and she was too tired to cook the eggs.

Rummaging around on the bottom shelf, she discovered a bag containing two slightly withered apples. She rinsed them both under the cold tap, then trailed out into the living room and flopped onto the convertible sofa, munching one of the apples without much enthusiasm.

She really ought to organize her grocery shopping and free time more efficiently, she decided. Although when she thought about it, she hadn't actually had much free time to organize over the past few months. Her evenings and even her weekends were frequently taken up attending media events arranged by the television studio or recommended by Damion's personal publicity consultants. Her lunch hours were consumed by business meetings.

Superficially her life seemed stuffed full of glamour. Old school friends called her occasionally, when they were passing through town, and she often invited them to come with her to some sophisticated Manhattan party. They always went away convinced that Lynn Frampton was leading the most exciting life of anyone they knew.

Ten months ago—three months ago—she would have agreed with them. But recently she had realized that attending parties, gallery openings, and gala first nights was exhausting when you went there to work and not to be entertained. It was her job to ensure that Damion was photographed talking with all the right people. It was her job to help him enhance his image as a serious actor. She spent hours propping up various bars, sipping club soda, and reminding reporters that Damion Tanner had several years of hard-won off-Broadway experience to bolster his current success as a television sex symbol. Casting directors, she had learned, had short memories and very limited vision even where superstars were concerned. They found it much easier to recall that Damion Tanner possessed a sexy body and a fabulous set of pectoral muscles than to remember his years of training as a serious actor.

The phone rang, and she stretched out impatiently to pick up the receiver. Tonight she wasn't in the mood to listen politely while somebody tried to sell her life insurance.

"Hello," she snapped.

"And a pleasant evening to you too, Lynn. I called to find out what time I should pick you up at the train station tomorrow."

She recognized the cool, faintly patrician voice immediately. "Adam!" she exclaimed. She put down her half-eaten apple and sat up straighter on the sofa, feeling a sudden surge of energy. "Adam, how terrific! Are you going to be in Bradbury tomorrow?"

"Naturally. How else could I meet you at the station?"

"I thought you were on the West Coast. Dad told me you had to fly out there three months ago, and I haven't heard a word from you since."

"I was on the West Coast, but now I'm back. I'm delighted to know you realized I was gone."

She heard a thread of laughter softening his normally cool voice, and for some reason, she felt warmed by his amusement. As she propped her feet up on a sofa cushion, some of the day's tension began to seep out of her tired muscles. It was always so *comfortable* to talk to Adam.

"Idiot! You've been my best friend for the last sixteen years at least. Of course I noticed you were gone."

"If I'd known you were missing me, I might have sent you a postcard." Before she could reply, he added, "Now that we've dispensed with protestations of undying devotion, do you think you could tell me what train you're catching? The seven-thirty or the nine o'clock?"

She felt a sudden sharp twinge of regret that her work for Damion was once again going to spill over into the weekend. It would have been nice to spend two whole days relaxing with Adam.

"I can't catch either of the early trains," she said, her voice soft with apology. "I have a few errands to run in the morning, but I'll try to catch the noon train; it gets into Bradbury at two-thirty."

"Can't you run your errands some other time? Your mother's already made blueberry crumble for lunch, and I have a new California recipe for ice cream— peanut butter and whiskey."

She laughed. "I'm almost relieved I won't be there. It sounds gross! I'll take care of everything as quickly as I can, I promise, but I have a couple of things I need to do for Damion."

"Ah, I see. For Damion. Naturally Damion's needs must come first. Well, make sure you get here by two-thirty, and if you're very nice to me, I may let you come fishing. I've got a pot full of squirming maggots waiting in your Dad's storage shed. You can bait my hook for me."

She laughed, thinking nostalgically of the many fishing trips she had taken with Adam and remembering her ghoulish interest in the wriggling bait worms.

"Hey, you're forgetting I'm not ten years old anymore," she said. "My childish interest in maggots has long since moved on to higher things."

"Yes, I know. When you were a kid, you were fascinated by night crawlers. Now you're fascinated by Damion Tanner."

There was a tiny pause, and then she gave a little

laugh. "Honestly, Adam, somebody ought to give you lessons in tactfulness! I don't think you realize what you just implied."

"Probably not. I was always better with numbers than with words." The clipped precision of his voice mellowed into tenderness. "You sound tired, Lynn. Why don't you get some rest, and I'll see you tomorrow?"

"I'm looking forward to it."

She smiled as she hung up the phone, feeling happier than she had all day. Dear Adam, she loved him so much. She was an only child, born when her parents were middle-aged and long since resigned to being childless, but having Adam Hunter for a friend was better than having an older brother. He teased her, laughed with her, listened to her. He loved her and cared for her, and he had never once let her down.

She had first met him seventeen years ago, during the summer that she turned nine. He'd been eighteen and, to her youthful eyes, already on the other side of the mysterious dividing line that separated grownups from children.

Her parents owned a successful country inn in northwestern Connecticut, and she was accustomed to a life that was full of people coming and going at short intervals. Being a naturally friendly child, she enjoyed meeting most of her parents' guests. She was especially interested in Adam, however, because her mother had mentioned that he was going to spend the whole summer at the inn and that his father would be coming up every weekend. Such long-term guests were a little unusual, and she soon guessed, with a flash of childish intuition, that Adam was unhappy. He always seemed to be hanging around the gardens doing nothing in particular. Lynn was a typically energetic nine-year-old, and sitting alone in the garden seemed a terrible waste of a hot summer.

The handyman, her special favorite among the hotel staff, had made her a small wooden box with a wire-mesh lid to use as a home for her family of pet snails. One particularly sultry afternoon when Adam had been at the inn for about a week, she went into the backyard to dig up some additions to her family. On her return to the house her concentration was so fixed on the giant snail she had captured that she walked straight into Adam.

"Oh, bother!" She peered anxiously into her box to make sure none of the snails had been disturbed. It was quite a while before she remembered her mother's instructions about being polite to the guests.

"I'm sorry," she said. "I wasn't looking where I was going. I hope I haven't made your clothes dirty."

"No, they're okay. Anyway, this is just an old shirt."

He still looked sad, she thought, and his gray eyes were kind of red and puffy. It bothered her to think he might have been crying. Everybody knew that grown-ups weren't supposed to cry. Especially boys. What could have happened to make somebody as big as he was start to cry?

"Would you like to see my snails?" she asked, doing her best to be friendly. Her mother couldn't stand the creatures, but her father didn't mind them too much, and the boys at school had all liked them a lot. Adam was taller than her father and broad in the shoulders, so he looked grown-up. But she decided that, where snails were concerned, he probably counted as a boy rather than a man.

"I have a big one in here with babies on its back," she said. "Do you think it's the mother?"

"No." He barely glanced at her grass-lined box.

"They're just part of the same colony. Snails are hermaphrodites."

"Herm . . . what?"

"Hermaphrodites." He looked at her impatiently. "They're both male and female at the same time. Or sometimes they change from one sex to the other. They start out as females and change to males as they get bigger."

She considered this startling piece of information in silence. It seemed incredible, but on the other hand, it certainly sounded interesting. She had thought all animals and insects had to be either boys or girls.

"Where do the babies come out from?" she asked, testing his knowledge.

He picked up one of the snails, and she noted approvingly that, unlike her mom, he didn't mind touching them. He pointed to the part she had thought was the head.

"Its reproductive organs are right up close to its mouth. This is the feeding organ, and the fertilized eggs come out of this little hole here."

Examining the snail closely, she decided that what he was saying might well be true. She decided to check out Adam's information with her father that evening. Dad would look it up in the encyclopedia for her if he didn't know the answer himself. Dad was big on looking things up in books. She put the snail back in the box and snapped the lid closed.

"Why are you sad?" she asked abruptly. "Don't you like it here? Most visitors think this inn is a pretty nice place."

As soon as she had spoken, she wished she hadn't. She knew that grown-ups didn't like you to ask personal questions, and she could see that her remarks had made him look more unhappy than ever.

"It's okay here," he said, his voice sounding hard and unfriendly.

"Well, that's good." She shifted uncomfortably from one sneakered foot to the other, rubbing her dirty hands against her skimpy cotton shorts. "I guess I'd better be going. My mom said I could help her make ice cream this afternoon."

He looked up suddenly, meeting her eyes for the first time. "My mother is dead. She died three weeks ago."

Lynn gulped. She had some friends whose parents were divorced, but she'd never met anybody whose mother had died. Most people she knew had grandmothers and several of her classmates had great-grandmothers. She didn't know what to say.

"I'm sorry," she mumbled. "That's terrible."

"She was killed by a burglar," he said, his voice sounding tight and full of rage. "She was shot by some crazy burglar who broke into our house. The police haven't found out who did it. My father says they probably never will."

Lynn thought about all the people she'd seen shot on TV or at the movies. Lots of blood spurted out when you were shot on television, but it didn't matter because you knew it was only paint or red makeup or maybe ketchup. Lynn tried to imagine her mother being shot for real, and even though she couldn't quite visualize the full horror of it, her stomach closed up into a cold, hard knot of pain.

"I'm sorry," she said again helplessly. She searched around to find some other words to explain to him how sorry she was, but her mind remained blank and her stomach sick with sympathetic revulsion. She didn't know how to put the words together to explain the way she was feeling.

"Would you like to come with me and make strawberry ice cream?" she blurted out, then could have kicked herself for asking such a dumb question.

"No, thanks." His face was closed and unfriendly.

She hadn't expected any other answer. She clutched her snail house closer to her ribs and pushed an untidy bunch of brown curls out of her eyes.

"Well, I've gotta get going," she said. "See you around."

"Yeah."

She was halfway to the back door when his voice reached her. "Wait!"

She turned slowly to look at him.

"I'm crazy about ice cream," he said. "Do the cooks get to taste what they're making?"

"Always." Her face split into a wide grin. "We have blueberries, too. Mom makes the best blueberry crumble in the whole world, and she's going to show me how to make it. You can taste that too, if you want."

It had been the first of many afternoons they spent together. That whole summer blended in Lynn's memory into one long, hot blur of sunshine as she and Adam explored the lush, green countryside together. She was desolate when he left for college in the fall, but to her delight, he returned to the inn almost every vacation, working as assistant handyman, waiting on tables, or serving drinks in the small bar. She was fifteen when he finally qualified as an accountant, but by that time his father had bought a weekend cottage in Bradbury, and she still saw Adam frequently.

The huge gap in their ages meant that their friendship had developed in a strange, lopsided fashion. Looking back with the perspective of an adult, she could see that, while she had confided totally in Adam, he had quite often only tolerated her company. Once she left for college, however, the difference in their ages had miraculously narrowed, and their friendship had undergone a subtle, undefined change.

Lynn tossed her apple cores into the garbage disposal and wandered into the bathroom to take a shower. It was curious, she thought as she lathered soap over her body, how in some ways she knew Adam so well and in other ways knew very little about him. Perhaps that was inevitable with the sort of close friendship they enjoyed. It was probably typical for brothers and sisters to feel both a deep intimacy and a slight barrier of reserve. She knew all his favorite foods, for example. She knew what books he liked to read and what movies he liked to see. She knew he liked Bach better than Beethoven and the Beatles better than Paul Simon. But she didn't really know much about his ultimate career goals, and she had no idea why he had never married, or even if he wanted to get married some time in the future.

She had a sudden vivid image of Adam married to one of the luscious lovelies who routinely paraded through his life, and she was aware of an irrational surge of pure jealousy. She laughed ruefully as she rinsed off the soap bubbles. Her jealousy was perfectly understandable, after all. She was wise enough to see that the peculiar closeness of her relationship with Adam would never survive his marriage.

Anyway, she didn't have to worry about the problem for a while since he wasn't likely to march down the aisle in the near future. Her mother was a lightning rod for information about impending weddings, and she hadn't breathed a word about any special woman in Adam's life.

Lynn hummed softly beneath her breath. The wonderful thing about her relationship with Adam was that, despite lengthy separations, the bond between them remained unbreakably strong. Even when their careers kept them on opposite sides of the country, a quick telephone call restored all the familiar sensations of closeness.

She wondered how long Adam would remain on the East Coast this trip. Her parents always sang his praises when she was home, telling her what a wonderful career he had carved out for himself. She didn't pay much attention to the specifics, but she felt a warm, absentminded pleasure that somebody so dear to her was apparently making such a success of his life.

She wasn't sure she could claim the same thing for herself. Professionally she was doing well, although not in the career she had originally chosen. She had majored in theater at Connecticut College but quickly realized that being the best actress at her local high school and third-best dancer in the college wasn't enough to cut it in the competitive world of professional acting.

It had been painful to accept her own relative lack of talent, but she prided herself on her common sense and quickly switched majors, taking a crash course in business administration during her final two years at college. To her surprise, she graduated almost at the top of her class. Still attracted to the world of the performing arts, she took a job in the New York publicity department of a major theatrical agency. She was so successful there that Damion Tanner's agent specifically sought her out for the job as Damion's personal manager and office administrator. Yes, she thought, professionally speaking, there was little doubt that she had arrived.

On a personal level, however, her life was about ready to qualify as a federal disaster area. She had fallen in love with Damion at their first meeting, and the more she saw him, the stronger her attraction had become.

Unfortunately he obviously didn't reciprocate her feelings, and she recognized that his complete indifference was beginning to have a depressing effect on all aspects of her life.

She had dozens of friends in Manhattan—she seemed to attract pleasant, kind, ordinary people with as much ease as Damion attracted supremely beautiful, supremely brainless young women. But recently she had found herself inventing excuses not to go out with her friends, even when she had a free evening. It was as if Damion's refusal to notice her as a woman was sapping her energy for all the other aspects of her life as well.

She had never told anybody, not even Adam, how she felt about Damion. She and Adam talked often about their personal feelings, but never about their love lives. Maybe this weekend she'd end her self-imposed silence. She'd reached the point where she felt desperate for some advice on how to break the ten-month-old stalemate. She had the wrong sort of personality for silent brooding, and she was far too energetic to relish drooping around, suffering from unrequited love. On the other hand, short of stripping naked and stretching out on Damion's king-size bed, she didn't know what more she could do to demonstrate that she was a desirable woman.

She stepped out of the shower and paused at the sink to brush her teeth. If anybody could give her advice on how to catch a man's eye, surely it would be Adam. He always seemed to have a harem of women clamoring for his attention. In that respect, if in no other, he and Damion seemed to have a great deal in common. This weekend, she resolved, she would get Adam in a quiet corner and find out what made him choose one woman over another.

She rinsed away the toothpaste and wiped the steam from the mirror to see her reflection more clearly. Men had often told her she was pretty, but that wasn't at all the same thing as being sexy. And where Damion Tanner was concerned, she had a feeling that *sexy* was an essential prerequisite to any relationship. She stared into the mirror. Medium-brown eyes, medium-brown hair, medium-pink skin. A medium-size head stuck on top of a medium-size body. She sucked in her cheeks, lowered her eyelids, and practiced looking sexy. The effort wasn't a success. She looked more like a cross-eyed pixie than a femme fatale. She'd have to ask Adam for some in-depth advice. It was a definite advantage to have an inside track on what was, so to speak, the opposition's point of view.

Lynn dabbed cream on the end of her nose, rubbed it across her cheeks, and gave up temporarily on the idea of looking sexy. This weekend she could afford to relax and enjoy herself. Monday would be time enough to put her new image into action, after she had absorbed Adam's expert advice.

Rummaging around in her dresser drawers, she unearthed a clean T-shirt to wear to bed, then opened up the sofa and climbed between the brightly patterned sheets. She must remember to ask Adam if it was true that most men found black satin negligees the ultimate turn-on. She pictured herself climbing into Damion's waterbed, clad in slinky black, but she couldn't bring the fantasy into proper perspective. Rolling sleepily onto her stomach, she decided that bouncy brown curls and five-feet-five-inch bodies didn't fit very well inside black satin.

There was no other reason she could think of why her fantasy remained so maddeningly out-of-focus.

CHAPTER TWO

SHE SAW ADAM as soon as the train pulled into Bradbury station. He was waiting by an old maple tree, leaning against a sleek, silver Pontiac Firebird, and reading a magazine. Some quirk of the afternoon sunlight as it filtered through the blazing autumn foliage cast his face into shadow, and for one disconcerting moment, Lynn had the impression she was watching a stranger. It was a long time since she had really looked at Adam, and she'd forgotten how tall he was and how powerfully built. She'd certainly forgotten the startling fairness of his hair and how sharply the golden color contrasted with the dark tan of his skin. He had spent the past three months working in California, and it showed.

The train stopped, and she walked slowly across the tracks, her steps almost hesitant. It was absurd, unbelievable, but she was suddenly shy at the prospect of meeting him again.

Looking up, he saw her at once, and waved in welcome. He tossed his magazine carelessly into the car and strode swiftly to meet her.

"Hello, Lynn. It's been too long since we got together." He brushed a light kiss against her cheek as he took possession of her small suitcase. "I like your outfit. That color suits you."

She sighed with silent relief when he placed his hand beneath her elbow, and her fleeting impression of Adam as a stranger changed back into the comfortable image she was accustomed to. She glanced down at her thick yellow sweater and pushed her hands into the pockets of her slacks as she twirled around for his inspection.

"You don't think these pants are too baggy? I'm not sure about this craze for pleated pants. You need to be a beanpole to carry them off properly."

He opened the car door and put her suitcase on the back seat, his gaze quietly mocking. "Are you asking me if your hips look fat, Lynn?"

She laughed. "I guess so."

"Well, the answer is no. They look enticingly rounded."

"Drat! I knew it! That means I have to lose five pounds at least."

"It depends on whether you're trying to impress other women or look good for the men in your life. Men would say you have a perfect figure."

"But I want to look good to other women, of course," she said, sliding into the seat next to his. "Don't you know that it's one of those self-serving male myths that women dress to please men?"

"Two minutes and thirty seconds," he murmured, putting the car into gear.

"What does that cryptic comment mean?"

"You were with me two minutes and thirty seconds before you delivered your first feminist lecture. I guess I should be grateful. That's probably a minute and a half improvement over the last time we were together."

She grinned. "If you weren't such a relentless chauvinist, I'd leave you alone. Look at this car, for heaven's sake! It practically shrieks 'Admire me. I'm a male potency symbol.'"

"At least it's not red."

"That just shows you're getting more sophisticated as you get older. You've reached the age when you know signs of virility can be effective even if they're kept a little bit subtle."

He sighed. "I knew I should have hidden this darn car in a barn and rented a station wagon for the weekend! If I pin a badge on my sweater saying that I think all housework should be done by men, that I approve of equal pay for comparable work, and that I think the next President of the United States should be a woman, will you stop nagging me about my Firebird?"

"I guess so, since you're a special friend, although it's probably violating my principles. I don't think your badge would be sincere."

He slanted a teasing glance at her through narrowed eyes. "You're growing up, Lynn. That's the first time I've ever heard you agree to a compromise."

"Youthful idealism fades fast in Manhattan. And I've been there four years."

There had been more cynicism in her voice than she intended, but Adam was tactful enough to make no comment. He swung the car into the narrow lane that led up to her parents' inn.

"So how have things been at work recently? Is Damion Tanner still as wonderful a boss as ever?"

"His show's still rated number one, which is extraordinary after three seasons. We're frantically busy, of course, but it's fun." She knew this wasn't the right moment to start talking about her one-sided love affair with Damion. She needed more time and Adam's undivided attention for that.

"How about you?" she asked. "How's your father?"

"Keeping fit and enjoying his retirement. I was afraid he might get bored, but he's agreed to sit on two or three charity committees, and he says he's busier now than he was when he was getting paid to work."

Adam slowed the car, then pulled into the tree-shaded parking lot of her parents' inn. She opened the door and breathed deeply. She could almost taste the crisp air tingling on her tongue. "I think October is my favorite month for coming here," she said.

"Yes, it's beautiful, isn't it? Some of the trees look like captured bursts of sunshine. I've found that one of the disadvantages of living in a big city like New York or Los Angeles is that you scarcely notice the change of seasons."

"There speaks a typical Angeleno! Tell that theory to a New Yorker trudging through two feet of snow when the buses have stopped running or sweltering through a July day when the office air conditioning has expired!"

Adam's laughing response was lost in the noisy welcome accorded to Lynn by her parents and the three family dogs, elderly mutts of doubtful origin who tried to prove they were still puppies by jumping up, barking hysterically, and winding their way through the maze of human feet.

Lynn's parents were delighted to see her. They kept her talking all afternoon and right through dinner, although it had been only a month since her last visit.

Lynn's mother was fascinated by Damion Tanner's television series and didn't hesitate to admit that she had fallen in love with the dashing Vietnam-veteran-turned-private-investigator whom he portrayed. She enjoyed hearing every snippet of insider gossip that her daughter could drag up. Lynn suspected that even her father, though he didn't talk much, had a sneaking admiration for Damion's insouciant wit and his daring rescues of innocent maidens in dire peril.

It was only after her parents had retired early to their bedroom for a good night's sleep that Lynn was able to get Adam alone and ask him the questions that had been uppermost in her mind ever since his telephone call.

She curled up on a corner of the sofa in the family's private sitting room and patted the seat cushion next to her. Ignoring her invitation, Adam walked over to the corner bar and poured himself a Scotch. He added ice cubes, but no water or soda, stirred the mixture briefly, and took a very long swallow.

"Um . . . Adam," she said, gathering her courage. In the privacy of her bathroom she had foreseen no difficulty in asking for his advice on how to attract Damion, but the reality of the situation was turning out to be rather different from her fantasy. The silence between them seemed strained, and she found the unusual tension totally unnerving. She and Adam *never* felt tense in each other's company, for heaven's sake.

"Adam," she repeated, then once again floundered to a halt.

"What is it?" he asked softly, not turning around.

She drew in a deep breath. "I have to ask your advice about something, Adam. I need your help."

He finally turned to face her, but his expression was obscured as he took another swallow of whiskey.

"Must be something serious," he said lightly. "You

haven't asked my advice about anything important for at least six years."

Her eyes widened in surprised denial. "I discussed all my college courses with you," she said. "And all my job applications. You were the first person I called when Damion offered me the job as his office manager."

"Yes, that's true. You've always kept me informed about the decisions you were making."

Her conscious mind scarcely registered the subtle distinction he had made. "I told you about my friends, too, even though you were so mean about them all." She grinned at a sudden memory. "Do you remember when you told me Mike Harmon was a turkey who only wanted my body and didn't appreciate my sensitive soul?"

"Was I right?"

"Good grief, Adam, the guy was captain of the ice hockey team, the biggest star of the drama class, and president of the Student Union. Every girl on campus wanted to go out with him, and you expected me to worry about whether we were soulmates! How could you have been so unfeeling? No wonder I gave up confiding my girlish secrets to you—if I did."

He turned back to the bar and added another cube of ice to his drink. "That was probably a wise move on your part. My advice might have been suspect."

She regarded him with affectionate accusation. "I think you must have taken your role as honorary elder brother a bit too seriously. It wasn't only poor old Mike Harmon who failed to pass muster as far as you were concerned. I seem to remember that you considered *all* my college boyfriends to be turkeys. Even Peter Grant, and he was Mom's absolute favorite. She was ready to call in the wedding caterers after the first weekend Peter spent here, but do you remember what you told me about him?"

"No."

"You said he seemed a charming, intelligent young man and that he obviously agreed with your flattering assessment!"

She expected Adam to respond with a teasing, light-hearted rebuttal. Instead, he looked at her long and hard, his gray eyes bafflingly introspective. "I shouldn't have said that," he said finally. "I have absolutely no right to pass judgment on your friends."

He walked over to the empty fireplace, finishing his drink in a single swallow. "But I don't think my uncalled-for advice made any difference to you, did it, Lynn? You slept with Peter Grant anyway. You were a virgin when you asked my opinion about him. You weren't when you came home for your next vacation."

His words were a flat statement, not a question. Even so, she felt her cheeks darken with embarrassed color. Adam had never before made any sort of comment, not even an oblique one, about her sexual behavior. Not that there was much for him to comment about. During her final year at college she had thought for a little while that she might be in love with Peter Grant, and they had conducted a tentative affair, full of youthful intensity and practical inexperience. They had continued to see each other when they both moved to New York, but their relationship had never grown into anything deeper, and they had parted without rancor months before she started working for Damion.

Her sexual experiences with Peter Grant, limited as they were, represented the sum total of her first-hand knowledge on the art of conducting a love affair. No wonder she needed advice on how to attract Damion

Tanner, she thought wryly. For a twenty-six-year-old woman living alone in Manhattan, she probably held some kind of chastity record.

She realized suddenly that Adam was watching her and that she was twisting one of her curls tightly around her index finger. She stopped the childish gesture immediately, annoyed at the nervous tension it revealed.

"Hey, what is this?" she asked with false brightness. "A grown-up version of show and tell?"

"No." His eyes sparked with sudden amusement. "I'm too smart to start that sort of parlor game. What would I do when it was my turn?" He poured himself another drink and sat down on the sofa, his arm stretched casually along the padded back. "So tell me what the problem is, Lynn. If I can help, you know I will."

She cleared her throat. She was finding this conversation more difficult by the minute, and so far they hadn't even said anything specifically about Damion.

"I want to make Damion Tanner notice me as a woman," she said at last, the words tumbling out in an embarrassed rush. "I want him to stop thinking about me simply as a professional who does a terrific job of organizing his business affairs. I want him to take me out, not just for business lunches, but someplace where he has a chance to get to know me as a person. I'm tried of having him look through me or over me or whatever the heck it is that he actually does. I want him . . . I want him to become my lover."

As soon as she finished speaking, she wished she could disappear into the sofa stuffing. She discovered—a little too late—that however long you'd known somebody, there were some subjects that remained too intimate to discuss.

"I find it hard to believe that Damion Tanner hasn't

already noticed you're a woman." Adam's voice was its most dry, but she perked up a little when she realized that he didn't sound either shocked or disgusted, merely exceptionally self-controlled.

"Well, I can assure you that he hasn't," she said gloomily. "Sometimes I think he sees me as a cross between a schoolteacher who keeps nagging him about his homework assignments and a personalized computer system that keeps his mail and contract commitments up to date. My secretary is great at her job. She also happens to be fifty-five years old, two hundred pounds, and a contented grandmother. If Damion's noticed any physical difference between us, he's keeping his awareness well hidden."

"Are you sure he isn't gay?"

She smiled without much humor. "Quite sure. Believe me, his male hormones all function on overdrive most of the time."

"And you want to become part of the crowd? One more forgettable item in Damion Tanner's collection of women?"

"No, of course not!" She drew her fingers over the quilted outline of a peony on the back of the sofa. "I've explained things badly, Adam. The problem is, Damion's so pleased with all the organization I've brought into his life that he doesn't stop to look at the woman behind the managerial skills. If he'd only take me out once or twice . . . if he'd only make love to me, I know our relationship would become something special. Damion is notorious for having affairs with his leading ladies, but he never dates an actress whom he admires. It's as if he's afraid of becoming involved with a woman who would demand his respect. But I think he likes me, and that fact alone would be enough to make our relationship different."

Adam's laugh was curiously tight. "Are you telling

me that Damion insists on seeing you simply as a good friend and you wish he wouldn't? You want him to see you as a woman and as a potential lover."

"Yes, that's exactly the problem." She sighed with relief at his understanding. "How in the world can I persuade him to see me in a different way, Adam? How can I show him that we could be lovers as well as friends?"

His gray eyes assumed the harsh, impenetrable gleam of polished steel, and once again she had the eerie feeling that she was seated opposite a virtual stranger.

"I'm not sure I'm the right person to advise you, Lynn."

"But there's nobody else," she said, shaking off her lingering misgivings. "Adam, you're my best friend in the whole world. Please, you can't let me down!"

The silence stretched out far longer than she thought it should before Adam finally replied. "Are you by any chance dreaming of orange blossoms and white lace, Lynn?"

She was shocked at the question. "I haven't really thought about it," she said. Somehow she had never considered how her relationship with Damion might develop. She had never allowed her imagination to stretch much beyond the magic moment of their first real date.

Adam regarded her closely, and she blushed. "Well, I guess I do think Damion needs a wife. Beneath all his surface success I think he's often a little lonely. And we do have a lot in common, you know."

"Do you?"

"Our interest in the theater, in movies, that sort of thing. I did train as an actress, after all. And Damion is a wonderful actor, one of the best."

"Oh, I see."

Adam got up, striding with sudden restlessness to stare out of the window into the blackness of the inn's deserted gardens.

"I don't know what you want me to say, Lynn. You're not a college student any more, and I have no right to pass judgment on your morals or on your choice of lovers. I'm not your father, and I'm not your older brother, although God knows you often seem to forget that. Do you want me to agree with you that Damion is a terrific actor? If so, I will. I've no doubt he'll collect a string of Oscars before his acting career is over. Do you want me to tell you he would be a great lover? Okay. From what I've seen on television, he looks like he would be fantastic in bed. I would guess he's every woman's dream of the perfect macho hero."

He shoved his hands into the pockets of his jeans, and the thick knit of his sweater suddenly stretched tight across his broad back.

"Do you want me to wish you a good time in his bed?" he asked, his voice harsh and unbelievably cold. "Okay. For what they're worth, you have my good wishes. I hope he lives up to every one of your fantasies."

It wasn't at all the way she had imagined he would respond. The cutting edge of his words transformed her request for advice into something sordid rather than amusing. She realized she felt faintly sick.

Adam's voice broke into the painful silence. "I gather I haven't said the right things. Or at least not the things you wanted to hear."

She hesitated before replying. The conversation had suddenly drifted so far out of her control that she couldn't quite think how to pull it back on track again.

"I was—I was really hoping for some practical advice, Adam, not a discussion about Damion's qualities as a lover. I know how successful you are with women."

His quick, hard laugh interrupted her. "Am I?"

"Of course you are," she said impatiently, dismissing his question. Adam's retinue of women had been legendary from the time he started college. "I thought you would be the perfect person for me to ask, partly because we're friends and partly because you're so well qualified to tell me what men look for when they're . . . when they're choosing a new lover."

"A lot of the time men aren't looking for anything more than a willing body. If you think one quick toss in the sack will be enough to change Damion's opinion of you, all you need to do is take off your clothes and lie down on the nearest bed or couch. I'm sure Damion will be delighted to oblige. Any normal man would."

This time there was no mistaking the note of cruelty in Adam's voice, and she was deeply hurt by it. She was shocked that he could misunderstand her so completely and dismayed that she had obviously expressed herself so badly. She had been asking for advice on winning Damion's love. Adam was acting as though she merely wanted a sexual tumble with a famous media personality. She swallowed hard, fighting back an unexpected rush of tears.

"That wasn't quite what I meant," she said, trying to smile as she uncurled herself from the sofa. "But for some reason, Adam, I have the feeling we're not communicating too well tonight. I think I'll say good night, and I'll see you tomorrow morning when we're not so tired. Are you still planning to go fishing?"

For a long moment he didn't move from his position by the window, and she had a curious, fleeting impression of incredible tension as he leaned his forehead against one of the darkened windowpanes. Then he turned around to look at her, and it was as if the preceding few minutes had never occurred. His smile contained all the warmth she was accustomed to seeing, and his eyes reflected a gleam of ruefulness.

"I'm sorry, Lynn. I've been behaving like a bear with a sore paw this evening. It's been a rough week for me. Could we start this discussion over, do you think?"

The thin layer of ice that had encircled her heart melted, and she immediately returned his smile. A twinge of common sense, however, warned her that she had made a mistake in asking for Adam's help with this particular problem. She had no intention of compounding the error.

"I think I asked you for the impossible," she said, forcing herself to sound a great deal more casual than she felt. "It was absurd to imagine that you could tell me how to attract another man's attention. I guess desperation addled my wits." She smiled at him, so that he wouldn't have to take her remarks too seriously.

"It wasn't so absurd," he said quietly. "You're a very pretty and likable woman, Lynn, so if Damion hasn't noticed you, there must be specific reasons why not. Perhaps he's never seen you in the right setting. I imagine he's only seen you in the office?"

She sighed. "That's not quite true. He often asks me to make up a threesome when he has to attend a movie premiere or a studio party, so he's seen me in informal settings. And I know he's dated other women he first met on a professional basis, so why am I different? Damion and I spend hours alone together organizing the details of his career. He respects my judgment. He values my opinion. How come he's never once thought it might be fun for us to go out together on a personal basis?"

"The problem is that you not only radiate efficiency, you also radiate wholesomeness." Adam's eyes gleamed with sympathetic amusement. "Let's face it, Lynn. You look so fresh-scrubbed and healthy that anybody seeing you immediately starts thinking about country gardens and fresh roses. Neither of which has much to do with dark Manhattan bedrooms and black satin sheets."

"How did you know Damion has black satin sheets?"

"I took a wild guess," Adam said, his tone drier than ever. "Taking another guess, I'd say that for Damion's taste a woman needs to look shadowed under the eyes, sultry around the mouth, and generally a touch world-weary."

"I already practiced looking hollow-cheeked and sophisticated in front of the bathroom mirror," Lynn confessed. "I just looked ridiculous." She ran her hands through her curls, clenching her teeth in irritation. "How can I look sophisticated and world-weary when my hairstyle comes straight out of a Shirley Temple movie? I bounce every time I move!"

"And not just your curls, either," he murmured.

She pummeled him with a convenient pillow. "One more remark like that, old friend, and I'll tell Mom that we *both* want lettuce leaves and lemon juice for lunch tomorrow." She stood up and walked across the room to stare at her blurred reflection in the darkened windows. "Oh, *hell!* I knew I had to lose five pounds."

Adam was suddenly behind her, his hands resting lightly on her shoulders. "Lynn, don't be ridiculous. You have a wonderful body."

"Then why doesn't he notice me?"

"If you want Damion to see you as a potential lover, you'll have to look the part. You'll have to look like a sensuous, sexually exciting woman. You'll need to look sexually aware."

"Instead of like a high school cheerleader, you mean." She tugged angrily at a strand of hair, then watched in the window as it sprang back into a soft curl against her cheek. "Sometimes I wonder if I'll still look like a healthy virgin when I hit my ninetieth birthday."

"If you do, console yourself with the thought that you'll die rich. You'll be able to make a fortune marketing your secret formula!"

"It's no laughing matter, Adam. Seriously, what do you suggest I do to change my image? Dye my hair platinum? Have it straightened? Get colored contacts so that I have mysterious green eyes instead of boring brown ones?"

He turned her gently around to face him. "You have superb eyes, Lynn, and fantastic hair. You just have to develop the right sort of face to go with them."

"What sort of face, other than clean-cut and wholesome, fits underneath a mass of brown curls?"

"A face that's provocative, earthy, and sexually aware."

She gulped. "I don't feel very earthy, Adam. And I don't feel even a little bit provocative. In fact Damion spends so much time looking through me, I've had days recently when I felt invisible."

Adam frowned. "It sounds to me as if you're suffering from an advanced case of destroyed self-confidence."

Before she could comment, he tilted her chin up and regarded her thoughtfully. "The right makeup could make a dramatic difference in your overall appearance," he said. "Fortunately you ought to be an expert on makeup after all those years of high school and college drama productions."

"I suppose mauve mascara and gray eyeliner might

help," she agreed. "And pouting lips outlined with dark lipstick and kept permanently shiny with lip gloss."

"Sounds as if you're getting the right idea. Try it out tomorrow, and I'll tell you if it works. From the consumers' point of view, that is."

"You'd better come to my room. If Mom or Dad saw me they'd probably have a heart attack. They both belong to the generation which thinks that a bit of pink lipstick and a dab of powder is all the makeup a nice girl ever needs."

"All right." He dropped his hands from her shoulders and returned to the bar, although he didn't pour himself a drink. He fiddled with the ice tongs for a while and then said, "Different makeup and new clothes will help, but it won't be enough, you know, Lynn."

"I realize that, but at least it's a start, and I'm grateful for your advice. I allowed myself to get so hung up about the way I look right now that I gave up thinking about how easily I can change my appearance. Women are transforming themselves every day, and there's no reason why I can't change, too."

"A new image will help, but what you really need is an exciting new lover." Adam propped himself casually against the bar. "You need somebody who'll make Damion jealous enough to sit up and take notice of what he's missing. There's nothing like some competition to get the old male hormones thumping."

"That might be a good idea, but it wouldn't work for me," she said softly. "I couldn't make love with one man just to make another man jealous."

Adam shrugged. "So find somebody who'll make Damion jealous but doesn't insist on going to bed with you."

"That's great in theory," she said, "but it's an impossible suggestion in practice. My supposed lover would have to be an extremely successful man if he's going to make Damion jealous, and where on earth would I find him? Eligible bachelors aren't exactly lurking on every Manhattan street corner, waiting to be picked up. And even if I did manage to find an eligible bachelor, why would he take me out and play the part of a devoted lover without expecting to share my bed? What would be in it for him?"

"You've forgotten something. You don't have to search for your eligible bachelor. You have me."

"You!" She was stunned by the suggestion. "But you're my *friend*, Adam. We're old friends from way back."

"You know that, and so do I. But does Damion?"

"Well, no, of course not. I mean, there's never been any reason to explain our relationship to him."

"Then it seems to me that you've just acquired a new lover." He walked across the room and caressed the curve of her cheek, his eyes teasing. "We've had such an incredible Saturday together, darling, that I can't imagine what the rest of tonight's going to be like. Is it bedtime yet? I've decided my patience is running out."

Feeling an odd tingle where his fingers rested against her jaw, she stirred uneasily beneath his laughing gaze. "Oh, come on, Adam, don't be crazy. You know it wouldn't work."

"Why not? Are you suggesting that I'm not successful enough in my chosen career to arouse Damion's spirit of competition?"

"You know that isn't what I mean. Mom and Dad are always telling me you'll be a millionaire by the time you're forty."

"They're wrong," he said lightly. "I'm already a millionaire, Lynn."

"Are you really?" For a moment her attention was

diverted. "I'm impressed. I always thought account-
ants managed other people's fortunes. I didn't know
they made fortunes of their own."

"I'm more a financial analyst than an accountant,"
he said. "And I've made some successful investments
in California real estate. That's why I've been spending so much time on the West Coast."

"However you've done it, there aren't many men
of your age who are self-made millionaires. You must
have been doing something right, Adam."

"I guess so. Anyway, am I successful enough to
take care of your objections?"

"You know it isn't your career that bothers me or
how successful you are. It's the idea of you and me
pretending to be lovers. That's a . . . well, it's kind
of . . ." She turned abruptly away. "It's a dumb idea,
Adam. Anybody looking at us would see that we're
just good friends. Nobody would ever believe that
we're in love."

"You were trained as an actress, so act. Pretend
that you're in love with me. Would that be such a
difficult thing to do?"

Her hands had somehow got themselves twisted
into a knot so tight that her knuckles were gleaming
white in the lamplight. She hastily unwound her fingers, wrapping her arms around her body in an in-
stinctively defensive gesture.

"It isn't only me who would have to pretend," she
said. "It's you, too. You've never had any professional training, so you'd never be able to act like my
lover. It's no good if I look all dreamy-eyed, and you
look at me just the way you usually do."

"And how is that, Lynn? Just how do I usually
look at you?"

"Well, you know. Sort of brotherly. Like a friend.
Dammit, Adam, that's what we are, so of course that's

how we look at each other!"

"I think you're underestimating my acting ability. If you like, I'll prove to you that I can play my part very convincingly."

"No, that isn't necessary, Adam. You know the idea would never—"

Before she could say anything further, he had circled her waist with his hands, drawing her tightly against his body. He bent his head to the nape of her neck and all at once—shockingly—she felt his lips move caressingly against her throat.

He pressed a kiss into the hollow at the base of her neck, and she jerked around in his arms, shivering with stunned disbelief when she felt his tongue flick briefly against her skin. He lifted his head, and his gray eyes, normally so clear and cool, seemed to burn with desire while his mouth was tight with a passion that seemed to be held barely in check.

She wanted to walk away, but her body had lost the power of independent movement, and she stared as if hypnotized when he bent his head again and captured her lips in a hard, angry kiss.

For several seconds she was too astonished to feel anything. Then an extraordinary quiver of sensation rippled down her spine, and before she had time to analyze what she was doing, her lips parted to accept his kiss.

His arms immediately tightened around her waist, and her heart began to pound with a frantic, thudding rhythm. His tongue pressed insistently against hers, and her arms clung to his neck as she automatically leaned more closely against him. His hands traveled down her back, molding her to his hips.

"I want you," he murmured, the words scarcely more than a whisper against her mouth.

"No!" She whirled away, finally regaining control

over her reeling senses. Oh, God! She must have slipped into a moment of temporary insanity.

"Adam," she whispered, "Adam, what happened to us? Have you gone crazy? What were we *doing?*"

"We were demonstrating that I'm quite capable of acting the part of your lover."

"Acting?" The astonished word emerged before she could pull it back. She turned to look at him, her arms clutched around her waist. He was pouring himself a club soda, and as far as she could judge, he looked exactly the same as he usually did: cool, controlled, and faintly sardonic.

She sank onto the sofa, hoping against hope that he wouldn't notice her burning cheeks. "You were acting?"

"Of course I was. Lynn, what is this? I was simply trying to reassure you by demonstrating that I'm quite capable of acting the part of your lover."

She stared at her knees as if she had never seen them before. "You looked . . ." She swallowed hard. "You looked aroused."

"I was," he said calmly. "I thought about a woman I really wanted to make love to, and then I kissed you. I was under the impression actors were taught to do things that way. Isn't it called displaying transferred emotions?"

She ignored his comments. "I don't think this is going to work, Adam."

"Nonsense," he said briskly. "Do you want to get Damion to notice you or not? Do you want him to become your lover? Because if you do, it's obvious that you're going to need my help."

"Well, I want him to fall in love with me. Of course I do."

Adam walked across the room and patted her affectionately on the back. "That's the spirit. We'll start work on your new image tomorrow. Do you know, I'm beginning to look forward to this whole project."

"Are you?" For some reason Lynn felt like crawling into a small, dark hole and bursting into tears, but Adam's smile brimmed with good humor.

"I'll come to your room after breakfast, and we'll begin with the makeup. It's going to be fun watching you turn into a whole new woman. I have a feeling that by the time we're through you'll be a five-feet-five-inch package of sexual dynamite."

She managed to return his smile. Adam was going to help her acquire a sensuous new image and attract Damion's attention. She knew she ought to be grateful to him. It was, after all, exactly what she had hoped for when she started this discussion.

She stared down at her knees again, wondering why her legs were still shaking. Why couldn't she meet Adam's eyes?

She decided it was bedtime. "I'm terribly tired," she said as she sprang to her feet and edged crablike toward the door. "I think I'll say good night, Adam."

"Good night, Lynn."

She didn't look at him when he answered her, and as soon as she reached the corridor, she fled to the safety of her room.

CHAPTER THREE

LYNN SET HER alarm clock half an hour earlier than usual on Monday morning so that she'd have plenty of time to work on her new image. Ever since she had been forced to give up the idea of becoming an actress, her makeup had consisted of nothing more than a dash of lipstick across her mouth and a quick flick of mascara on the tips of her lashes, but she realized her new image was going to take considerably more effort to produce.

She scowled as she passed the bathroom mirror and caught sight of her tousled curls and pink cheeks. An extra half hour didn't look like it was going to be long enough, she thought pessimistically.

She set coffee to percolate while she showered, then wrapped herself in a towel and carried a mug of coffee into the bathroom. Her supply of new makeup, bought yesterday morning with Adam's help, was already spread out over the counter next to the sink. She dubiously examined the pots and jars, then patted tinted foundation onto her cheeks and stroked a delicate lavender eye shadow across her lids. She peered into the mirror, examining the effect. Maybe Adam was right. The mauve shadow did seem to make her eyes look larger and more mysterious. Satisfied, she hummed under her breath as she cautiously highlighted her cheeks with blusher.

Brushing dark plum lip gloss onto her mouth, she thought about the time she had spent yesterday with Adam. After buying the makeup, they had locked themselves in her bedroom, and she had been overcome with an impulse to giggle as they experimented with one exotic color scheme after another. She'd been grateful to him for the deliberate casualness of his manner, and even more grateful for all the practical advice he'd given her. By teasing her and mocking himself, he'd managed to turn what could have been embarrassing into a few hours of almost adolescent fun.

But back in her own apartment, in the cold light of a Monday morning, Lynn couldn't believe she had actually told him the truth about her feelings for Damion. In retrospect she wondered if she had temporarily blown one of her mental circuits. There seemed to be no other explanation for her irrational behavior.

A strange tingle rippled down her spine as she thought about Adam's offer to play the part of her lover. The pot of lip gloss suddenly shook in her hands.

"Damn!" She wiped away a tiny smear of color from the corner of her mouth. The idea of Adam as her lover was ridiculous, of course, and she had no intention of taking him up on his suggestion. Adam was her friend, and despite what he had said, there was no way an old friend could suddenly smolder with fake sensuality. He would never be able to act well enough to carry off the deception—although his kiss had been pretty convincing. In some ways it had been altogether too convincing... She quickly snapped off the thought. For some reason she felt acutely uncomfortable remembering Adam's make-believe kiss.

She closed the lid on her blusher and cast a final glance into the mirror. She looked different, there was no doubt about it. She even felt different inside, as if she were hovering on the brink of a momentous self-discovery.

Grimacing at the fanciful thought, she hurried out of the bathroom. She didn't have time for self-discovery this morning. From her closet she took out a gray and white silk blouse and a straight gray skirt that was slit in the center to a point four inches above her knees. She examined the outfit thoughtfully, registering the fact that the somber colors only enhanced the low neckline of the blouse and the sleek, clinging lines of the skirt.

"You have fabulous legs," Adam had said yesterday, looking at them with the detached interest of a livestock judge inspecting a prize heifer. "You may as well display them to advantage. You should wear skirts more often, Lynn. Pants don't do you justice."

With a sudden, impatient shrug she threw the outfit onto the bed and banged the closet door shut. She would wear the darn skirt. If she was going to change her image, she might as well do a thorough job of it.

For once the morning traffic moved without a hitch, and it was only eight-thirty when she arrived at the office. Betty, her secretarial assistant, had already arrived, and she whistled appreciatively as Lynn walked into the room.

"Hey, you look terrific! What's the special occasion? Got a hot date at lunchtime?"

"Nothing so exciting," Lynn replied, trying to sound casual. The last thing she wanted was for Betty to suspect the humiliating truth about her unreciprocated feelings for Damion. "I just bought some new clothes, and I felt like wearing them, that's all. How was your weekend?"

"Horrible. Miserable. I'm on a diet."

"Oh, no, not another diet! Betty, I don't think I can stand the strain! It's only a month since you ended the last one. I still gag at the sight of cottage cheese, and I wasn't even eating it!"

"This is a different diet. No cottage cheese, I promise."

"So tell me the worst. What is it?"

"All the grapefruit I can eat for lunch and broiled chicken breasts for dinner."

"I hate grapefruit. Couldn't you just starve yourself on the weekends when I don't have to watch? I hate feeling guilty, and I know I ought to lose five pounds."

Betty snorted. "Where from? You don't have an ounce of excess fat anywhere."

"You're too kind, but I love to listen to you. What started this sudden compulsion to diet? You were quite happy with yourself and the world when you left here on Friday."

"My grandson wanted me to go bicycling with him on Saturday morning, and when I tried to fit into my stretch pants, I couldn't pull them past the bulge in my thighs. Every woman has her sticking point. For you it's probably a size eight. For me it's a size twenty."

Lynn laughed, and at that moment Damion walked out of his private living quarters into the office. Her gaze met his, and her heart pounded faster when she caught sight of his devastating blue eyes.

He smiled absently, not really seeing either of them. "Morning, Lynn. Morning, Betty. Could you retype these two pages of script for me, please? The director and the writer have made so many changes, I can't see what I'm supposed to say anymore."

"Certainly, Damion. I'll do it right away," Betty said.

He dropped the manuscript on her desk and turned to clap an arm around Lynn's shoulder.

"Well, babe, you're looking great," he said, giving her no more than a cursory glance. "How was your weekend?"

"It was excellent, thanks. An old friend flew in from an extended trip to California, and we had a good time together."

"That's terrific. Come into my sitting room as soon as you can, will you? Bob's already called from the coast. He wants my final reaction to that movie script, and I need to talk it over with you again before I give him my verdict."

He walked out of the room without so much as another blink in her direction.

She could have been dressed in a Salvation Army overcoat for all the notice he had taken of her, Lynn thought wryly. So much for slit skirts and elegant legs, not to mention plum-colored lips and purple eye shadow. Was she really so unfeminine? So totally unremarkable? She gathered up a notepad and some pencils, smothering a sigh as she followed him into his private suite. Dammit, she was going to make Damion realize she was a woman if it was the last thing she did.

They worked hard together all morning. They were alone most of the time, but Damion couldn't have paid her much less personal attention if she'd been a computer. In fact she could follow orders, make intelligent comments, and discuss the movie script without Damion ever needing to focus his dazzling gaze directly upon her.

He left the office at noon, saying that he planned to take Tiffany Brandon, the new female star of his television series, out for lunch. As far as Lynn was concerned, this brief announcement was the crowning touch to a wretched morning. Was he about to ditch Christine Mitchell, only to take up with another one of his leading ladies?

The door slammed shut behind him, and Betty winked conspiratorially. "Looks as if our dear friend Christine is on the way out. Can't say I'm sorry. She's not the most pleasant person to be around. Have you met Tiffany in person yet? Is she any better?"

"What? I'm sorry, Betty, did you ask me a question?"

"It doesn't matter, kiddo. Although I must say, for a woman who's wearing a spectacular new outfit supposedly for no special reason, you certainly seem to be a touch absentminded this morning. Are you sure nothing exciting happened this weekend? No devastating new man in your life?"

Lynn's laugh was tinged with a touch of hysteria. "No, I spent the weekend with a very old friend." With considerable effort she managed to refocus her attention on her work. "Are you planning to go out for lunch, Betty?"

"Yes, I am going to order my grapefruit and black coffee from the coffee shop on Madison. I thought it might seem like I was getting more food if I ate my meager allowance in a restaurant."

"Bring me back a container of mushroom soup, will you? I don't want to go out. I have a couple of things I need to finish up over the lunch hour."

"Sure. Why should I mind walking two blocks

smelling somebody else's delicious food when my stomach's rattling like a kettledrum?"

"But think of how terrific you'll feel next weekend when you fit into your jogging pants."

"Don't I wish! Knowing me and my metabolism, it'll probably be a month of starvation before I lose five pounds."

Lynn smiled sympathetically, but her mind wasn't really on her secretary's weight problem. She was thinking about the publicity party she was scheduled to attend with Damion that evening—in a working capacity, of course.

As soon as she was alone, she reached for the phone and without giving herself time to reflect, punched out the number of Adam's Manhattan office. So much for her firm determination not to involve him in her plans, she thought wryly.

She had to go through an operator, a secretary, and a male assistant before she reached Adam. His staff had obviously expanded considerably since the last time she phoned his office.

"Hello, Lynn. How are you?" His voice was friendly, as it always was whenever she called him, but she discovered that her hand was damp where it held the telephone. She must be nervous because of what she was about to ask him. There couldn't be any other reason for the sudden acceleration of her heartbeat. She cleared her throat.

"Hello, Adam. I'm fine. Um...how are you?"

"Busy, but pleased to be talking with you."

"Yes, well, I won't keep you more than a minute. The fact is, Adam, I—I was wondering if you were free this evening."

There was an infinitesimal pause. "I have a business dinner, but I guess I could adjust my calendar if it's important to you."

"It is rather important." She gulped. "Damion asked me to go to a party with him. It's a publicity affair organized by his studio. I guess it's going to be a spectacular event."

"He invited you to be his date for the evening?" Adam's question sounded surprisingly sharp.

"Oh, no! Tiffany Brandon will be his date. He's asked me to attend strictly for business reasons. He needs me there to help out his publicist."

"I see. I gather the new image didn't produce the effect you'd hoped for. I'm sorry."

"There's no reason to apologize. It's not your fault." She took her courage into both hands. "Adam, I remembered . . . I thought about what you said over the weekend, and I wondered if you would mind acting as my escort tonight. I know studio parties aren't exactly your scene—"

"It would be my pleasure," he said, cutting her off. "It sounds as if it might be a fun evening."

It wasn't exactly the response she had anticipated, and she wondered for a moment if he had misunderstood her invitation. "You remember what we were talking about this weekend, Adam? The thing is, I need your help."

"Don't worry. I understand perfectly that you've only asked me to go because you want me to play the part of your lover. I promise I'll be very attentive."

Lynn hoped Adam's secretary couldn't hear what he was saying. She wiped her palm on a tissue, wondering why her hand felt stickier by the minute, while Adam merely sounded faintly amused.

"Well—uh—thanks," she said. "I appreciate your help."

"Don't mention it. What time would you like me to pick you up?"

"Is eight o'clock convenient?"

"I'll be there. Good-bye, Lynn."

She was still staring at the phone, listening to the dial tone, when her secretary returned to the office.

"Here's your soup, kid. Never say I don't make sacrifices for my friends."

"Thanks, Betty." Lynn took the foam cup and swallowed a couple of sips. "Do you think you could take care of the office for a couple of hours this afternoon?" she asked. "I have to go shopping for a new dress. Don't worry about that huge pile of fan mail. I already checked through it, and most of it only needs one of the computerized form letters for a reply. I'll come in early tomorrow morning so you don't have to cope with it all."

"Sure, no problem. It's about time you took some time off, anyway. You've worked too many twelve-hour days recently." Betty sat down at her desk and regarded Lynn shrewdly. "What's the special occasion? Something exciting?"

Lynn was taking her jacket out of the coat closet and didn't turn around. "Oh, no special occasion, not really. Just another publicity party. You remember, it's the one the studio chief is throwing to celebrate the inauguration of Tiffany Brandon's role on Damion's series."

"And you need a new dress for that?" Betty didn't bother to conceal her disappointment. She was an inveterate matchmaker, and having successfully married off all three of her daughters, she was now determined to perform the same service for Lynn. She was forever trying to fix her up with one of the eligible bachelors who floated in and out of Damion's entourage.

Lynn knew perfectly well what her secretary was thinking, but she managed to produce a casual grin as she pulled on her jacket. "Sorry to disappoint you,

Betty, but this is strictly business. I'll be back by three, which should be at least half an hour before Damion gets through with his lunch date."

It took a while to find what she was looking for. After searching fruitlessly in a couple of big department stores, she went into a boutique on Fifth Avenue where one of the assistants wore skin-tight jeans and had striped pink and purple hair, and the other wore a sober black suit and had her gray hair twisted into a bun. Whatever their personal taste in clothing, they both knew their trade. After listening carefully to Lynn's requirements, they produced a heavy silk dress that was a masterpiece of understated seductiveness. Long and elegantly cut, it was designed to leave one shoulder and most of her back provocatively bare. The fabric was a shimmering, muted shade between bronze and gold. A slit on one side reached no further than mid-thigh, but because the dress was long, it created a distinctly erotic impression.

"You look totally awesome!" the striped-hair attendant said when Lynn emerged from the dressing room.

"It's very flattering, miss," said the gray-haired matron.

Lynn glanced over her shoulder at the floor-length mirror and secretly agreed. In her most optimistic fantasies she hadn't expected to look this good. Just wait until Damion saw her! Good lord, he probably wouldn't even recognize her. The fact was, she admitted wryly, she scarcely recognized herself.

She was halfway back to the office when she remembered that Adam was escorting her to the party; he, too, would see her in the dress. The realization caused a surprising wave of heat to wash over her body.

She wasn't at all sure why.

CHAPTER FOUR

LYNN WAS SHIVERING when she finished dressing that night, although she suspected that her trembling had little to do with the slight chill of the night air. She opened her closet door and took one last look in the mirror, trying to reassure herself that she didn't look like a teenager dressed up in her older sister's clothes.

The image reflected in the glass bore little resemblance to the rosy-cheeked, cherubic Lynn Frampton she was accustomed to seeing. She had pulled her hair back from her face, piling it on top of her head in a crown of soft curls. Antique earrings, studded with clusters of topaz, swayed against her neck, highlighting the golden texture of her skin and emphasizing the bare, tanned slope of her shoulders. The dress was designed with its own half-slip, and the low-cut bodice meant that she couldn't wear a bra. The heavy silk felt slippery against her naked breasts, and she knew without looking in the mirror that her eyes gleamed with an unfamiliar fire.

The intercom buzzed, and her stomach lurched when Adam's composed voice announced his arrival. It lurched again when the ring of the doorbell signaled his presence at her apartment door.

She opened the door. He was leaning against the corridor wall, startlingly good-looking in a dinner jacket and white pleated shirt. She realized with a slight shock that it had been years since he had escorted her somewhere that required formal clothes. Looking into his eyes, she saw for a split second the shadow of some intense emotion, then he blinked, and his patrician features displayed only the familiar warmth of long-standing friendship.

He straightened up from the wall. "Hello, Lynn," he said, smiling offhandedly as he walked into her apartment. "Hey, you look terrific! That dress is sensational; just what you need to impress Damion. You've certainly chosen well."

His silvery gaze ran over her in a cool, impersonal appraisal, and she felt her breath lock in her throat. She waited for him to say something—she wasn't sure what—but when he remained silent, she turned her back on him and walked hastily to the corner of the living room, where a bookshelf also served as a small bar.

"You're very punctual," she said, her fingers playing restlessly with the ice tongs. "What I mean is, I appreciate your offer to escort me tonight. I know how busy you always are when you're in Manhattan."

"It's my pleasure. Actually, I'm dying to meet Tiffany Brandon. She's been one of my secret heartthrobs for at least three years."

Her head jerked around. "I didn't know that."

He smiled. "No. But then we never have discussed my preferences in women, have we?"

"I thought that any woman who curved in the right places met with your immediate approval."

"You've been listening to my father," he said lightly. "You ought to know you can't believe everything parents say. When you were seventeen, for example, your mother told me you were madly in love with me. She felt obliged to warn me you were too young to know your own mind."

The ice tongs slipped from her fingers, rattling noisily as they fell. Her hand was suddenly covered in a hard, warm clasp.

"Don't be nervous," he said softly. "I'll play my part perfectly, Lynn. Damion will notice you tonight, I promise."

She gave a tiny sigh of relief. Of course! It was the prospect of the party that was setting her so much on edge. After all, a great deal was at stake. If Damion didn't notice her tonight, despite all Adam's advice and help, then she would have to accept that there was absolutely no hope for her. Adam was always so perceptive, she thought. It was typical that he should understand how she was feeling before she had even clarified it for herself.

"Would you like a drink?" She managed a bright smile, reassured by her own rationalizations. "I have Scotch, vodka, or white wine if you prefer it."

"I'll wait until I've eaten something at the party, thanks. I didn't have time for lunch, and I don't like to drink on an empty stomach."

His voice sounded relaxed, his gray eyes were guileless, and his expression was as jovial as she could have wished. She wondered why his cheerfulness made her feel vaguely angry. For a split second she was aware of an incongruous tension in the room, and she jumped when he rested his hand on her bare shoulder.

"I'm truly impressed, Lynn," he murmured. "I knew you could work wonders if you set your mind to it, but that dress is absolutely spectacular. How about turning around slowly so I can view you from all angles?"

"Very nice," he said, when she had complied with his request. "The color is really flattering to your hair. It brings out all the golden and chestnut highlights." To Lynn, his tone was reminiscent of a grandfather complimenting his young granddaughter on her new party dress.

"I'm glad you like it."

"Mmm . . . I like it a lot, but I think there's something wrong with the neckline. It doesn't seem to be draped properly at the front. There's a little bump, right in the middle."

With a casual smile he reached out and adjusted one of the low folds of the neckline, turning it inward against her skin. His fingers felt warm and firm as they brushed against the soft curve of her naked breasts, and her heart began to pound with the urgency of an overworked trip-hammer.

It seemed a long time before he finished his adjustments. After several rearrangements, he held her at arms' length and inspected his handiwork.

"That's better," he said. "It looks more provocative this way. You had it pulled up a fraction too high, and it ruined the effect."

She swallowed, trying to moisten her dry mouth. "Too high?" she finally managed to say. The words came out in an embarrassing, raspy squeak.

"Don't worry, it's all fixed now. Are you ready to go?"

"I just have to get my coat."

She darted toward the closet, relieved at the chance

to escape his inspection. She didn't know what was wrong with her, getting shaky at the knees simply because Adam touched her. Good grief, he must have touched her a thousand times in the years they had known one another. On fishing trips he had frequently hauled her bodily out of the water. She had no idea why tonight the delicate trail of his fingertips across her breasts had made her stomach clench tight with an almost unbearable excitement.

Lynn found her velvet evening coat and thrust her arms into the padded sleeves. "I'm all set," she said, trying to keep her voice every bit as nonchalant as his had been. "Shall we go?"

The pressure of his hand against her back was entirely impersonal as they rode down in the elevator and summoned a cab, and Lynn admitted to herself that Adam was handling this whole situation a great deal better than she was. She wondered why she was finding it so difficult to treat him naturally. She had been ill at ease with him ever since he suggested playing the part of her lover. The fact was, despite her training as an actress, she didn't seem to have his capacity for compartmentalizing the pretense and the reality.

As they drove downtown, he chatted amiably about his day in the office, and Lynn did her best to respond with equal nonchalance. By the time the cab drew up at their destination, she had decided that she ought to be grateful for Adam's relaxed manner and the casual way he had given his approval of her new dress and her changed appearance. Their real relationship, their long-standing friendship, was too important to damage for the sake of a temporary pretense. It was a good thing one of them seemed to be retaining a sense of perspective.

The party was only just beginning to get into its

stride when they arrived. The penthouse apartment belonged to Lionel Brede, the head of the studio producing Damion's television series, and he had designed the living room expressly as a backdrop for large parties. Lynn had been to the apartment several times before, but Adam looked around appreciatively when they walked in after handing their coats to a maid.

The main reception room was vast. One of the walls consisted entirely of glass, giving a glittering night-time view of the city, and the remaining walls were stark white, highlighting several vivid abstract paintings. The floor was black marble and the furniture was all scarlet. A white-draped buffet table was laden with untouched food—television cameras were merciless to people who carried excess pounds—but the three bartenders were working busily, even though the room was still only half-filled with guests.

Lynn spotted Damion almost at once. He was standing in front of the black marble fireplace, his magnificent body dramatically silhouetted against a blazing fire. He held a drink in one hand, and his other arm was draped around a willowy brunette with waist-length hair and an improbably large bosom. Lynn recognized the famous features of Tiffany Brandon. Damion was talking to a reporter, but he glanced frequently at his companion, and it didn't require exceptional powers of insight to see that he was finding her delightful company. Lynn stared at them both for several frustrating seconds, then tried unsuccessfully to smother a sigh.

Adam's hand immediately moved from its light clasp at her elbow and began moving on her back in a delicate caress. She stiffened and would have jerked away, but he pulled her against his side and bent down so that his mouth was close to her ear.

"I'm your lover, remember?" His voice was a husky whisper against her cheek. "Would you please turn around and look at me as if you can't wait to get me back in your bed?"

She gulped. "I c-can't do that, Adam. Besides, there's no need to pretend just yet. Damion isn't even looking in this direction."

"He is now. For goodness' sake, Lynn, cling to my arm and smolder."

Far from molding itself to his arm, her body seemed determined to give an expert imitation of a guardsman on ceremonial duty. "I can't look smoldering," she said despairingly. "And I can't cling. Not with *you,* Adam."

She wasn't prepared for the momentary fury that flared in his eyes. "Why not?" he asked tightly. "What's so different about me? I'm a perfectly normal male, with all the usual masculine components. I've even been told that some women find the thought of having me in their beds quite desirable."

"That's not the point, Adam."

"No?" Emotion darkened his eyes again, so briefly that she couldn't tell if it was anger or something else. "Let me remind you that the idea of this charade is to make Damion jealous. We can't do that very successfully if you won't even look at me."

Involuntarily her gaze flew once again to the marble fireplace. Damion was still staring in their direction, although he didn't betray any sign of recognition. Her brown eyes softened as he flicked an errant lock of hair away from his forehead, and she was unable to conceal another small sigh of longing.

With a sudden impatient exclamation Adam grasped her chin and forced her face around to his. Indifferent to the people milling around them, he held her still while he brushed a long, lingering kiss across her mouth.

When he finally let her go, she stared at him in silence, her eyes closing when he reached out and drew his thumb gently across her lips, touching where his mouth had touched, exploring the softness that his mouth had already felt.

She jumped at the sudden sound of his voice, her eyes jerking open. He was looking at her with a mixture of reproof and mild disapproval.

"You're really going to have to do a better acting job, Lynn. I can't pull this thing off all by myself, you know, and after all, you're supposed to be the one with professional training."

"W-what do you mean?"

He took two glasses of champagne from a passing waiter and handed one to her. She took a large swallow.

"To be perfectly honest, Lynn, your performance so far has been abysmal. It wouldn't deceive a babe in arms, let alone Damion Tanner. Try to remember that you're supposed to be in love with me. Touch me occasionally. Ruffle my hair and gaze longingly into my eyes. You're hoping to make Damion jealous, so for heaven's sake stop gawking at him like a lovesick teenager. I can't haul you into my arms and kiss you *every* time you start drooling over him. Apart from anything else, it'll ruin your new makeup."

"I wasn't drooling over him," she snapped. "He's not an ice cream cone. And anyway, I never asked you to kiss me. It was the last thing I wanted you to do."

"Now that's much better," he said with maddening superiority. "You're actually looking straight into my eyes, and your cheeks are flaming. I think you should aim for that sort of fiery expression when you introduce me to Damion. Your eyes have gone all smoky, you know. It's a terrific effect. Very sexy."

Discovering that her teeth were clenched together, she carefully unclenched them. "My eyes always change color when I'm angry," she said.

"So they do. I'd forgotten. You haven't been really mad at me since you were about sixteen and I refused to take you camping in the Adirondacks." He sipped his champagne thoughtfully. "Maybe I should concentrate on making you angry, since you're not very good at faking any other sort of passion toward me. We've got to do something to make old Damion sit up and take notice, and he probably wouldn't realize that you were vibrating with rage rather than sexual desire. I don't think he's the most perceptive of men, do you?"

"I don't know." She clutched her gold evening purse like a lifeline. "Adam, I always thought this crazy scheme was a disastrous mistake, and now I'm sure of it. I'm sorry, I know you're only trying to help, but I'm just not capable of acting the passionate lover with you when I'm really thinking about Damion."

"In my opinion, Lynn, you haven't even begun to learn what you're capable of doing," he said coolly. "If you find my attentions hard to take, just concentrate on dear old Damion, and I'm sure all your sacrifices will seem worthwhile."

She opened her mouth to protest again, but he crooked his index finger under her chin and gently closed her mouth. "I think I should meet Damion now, don't you? The reporter seems to have finished his interview, and we don't want to waste any more time. After all, we're here to create an impression, not to enjoy ourselves."

"I didn't know that's what we'd been doing," she muttered as he began to escort her briskly across the room. His fingers were splayed intimately against her waist, burning her skin through her silk dress. She tried to ignore his touch, telling herself it was a necessary part of the game they were playing, but she couldn't get the sensation out of her mind. Her skin had begun to feel as if it were on fire.

"Adam," she said finally, "your hand. You—um— have to move it."

He turned to look at her, then dropped his gaze to her waist. His body tensed, as if he was astonished to discover exactly where his hand lay.

"Oh, I'm sorry," he said. He slid his fingers up her ribcage until they were practically cupping her breast. "That was careless of me. I forgot that in the circles Damion moves in people are pretty demonstrative, even in public. Is that better?"

She gritted her teeth. "I didn't mean you had to move your hand *that* way," she said tersely. "I meant for you to take it completely away."

"That wouldn't look right," he said mildly. "We're supposed to be lovers, Lynn, not colleagues on the Sunday school teaching team. Don't get so uptight about trivia. What's a little physical intimacy between two old friends? Keep reminding yourself of your goal, and things will work out fine. Surely no sacrifice is too great if it enables you to attract dear old Damion's attention?"

"Why do you always sound so sarcastic when you mention his name?"

"I'm sure you've misunderstood me. Why should I be sarcastic about a wonderful fellow like Damion?"

She had no chance to pursue the subject, because at that moment they arrived at Damion's side. He was temporarily alone, Tiffany Brandon having retired to a corner of the room for a photo session. He greeted them politely, his professional smile firmly in place, his manner at its most charming as he ran an approving eye over Lynn.

"Hello, nice to see you both here. Are you from the network publicity—" Damion broke off in mid-sentence. *"Lynn!* Good lord, what have you done to yourself? For a moment I didn't recognize you. Damn, but you look wonderful, babe, simply wonderful."

The admiration in his husky voice was entirely genuine, and Lynn experienced a moment of supreme feminine gratification. At last, after all these months, he was really looking at her! And he was finding her attractive! His stunned reaction had been everything, and more, that she had ever dreamed of. Her eyes sparkled with happiness.

"Hello, Damion," she said, laughing softly. "I thought it was time I bought some new clothes. I'm glad you approve of my choice."

"Approve? That dress is fabulous! I never realized before what a terrific figure you have, Lynn babe." His eyes were hot as they roamed over her body.

"She knows how much I like to see her in that particular shade of gold," Adam interjected. His voice was as smooth as cream, but she was vaguely conscious of his hand tightening at her waist. "You chose that dress especially for me, didn't you, darling?"

"W-what? Oh, yes. Yes, of course."

Adam extended his right hand toward Damion. "I'm Adam Hunter," he said. "A very special friend of Lynn's."

He paused just long enough to allow the significance of the words to sink in, then he smiled. "I'm a great admirer of your television series, Mr. Tanner. It's one of the few weekly shows I make sure not to miss."

"That's good to hear," Damion said heartily. "It's tough for a show to remain number one in the ratings for more than a season, but we've managed to do it."

"Thanks largely to your brilliant acting, I'm sure."

Damion ran his fingers through the lock of dark, curly hair that had fallen back over his eyebrow. "It's true that I've won several awards," he said, looking modest. "The critic in the *Times* said only last week that it was my acting ability that held the show together."

"And I'm sure he's right. You're quite an actor, Mr. Tanner." Adam's voice lowered confidingly. "Of course, I've had another interest in the series apart from your own brilliant acting. As a—close—friend of Lynn's, I was naturally intrigued to see the man she works for."

Damion's eyes narrowed. "How long have you been Lynn's *close* friend? She's never mentioned you before."

"I expect it was too painful for her to talk about me while we were apart," Adam said. "I've been tied up on the West Coast putting together an important deal, and I only got back to New York at the end of last week. Lynn missed me a lot, and it was good to know she had her work with you to keep her occupied. We talked on the phone all the time, of course, but phone calls are no compensation for lack of physical contact, are they?" He turned and smiled sweetly at Lynn. "Isn't that right, darling?"

She had paid almost no attention to what Adam had said. She was floating on a cloud, drowning in the glorious depths of Damion's eyes. She recognized the subtle undercurrent of hostility flowing between the two men, and she reveled in the intoxicating knowledge that Damion was actually jealous.

"I'm sorry," she said, not even turning to look at

Adam. "What did you say?"

"I said you missed me desperately while I was on the West Coast. Isn't that right, *darling?*"

"Oh—uh—yes. Yes, absolutely. I missed you because you were away on the West Coast," she repeated dutifully.

At that moment the head of Damion's public relations agency walked up, which was probably just as well, Lynn acknowledged wryly. If this was the best she could do, no wonder she had flunked out of drama class.

"We need you for some publicity shots, Damion," the agent said. "We're planning to break the news that you and Tiffany are a hot item off the set as well as on it. We want to pose you with her for some shots that look as if you've been caught unaware. You know, hand in front of the face, your body half-shielding Tiffany's, that sort of thing. The public always prefers to think they're being let in on something secret. I've already drawn up a press release which says there's absolutely no truth to the rumor that you both spent a week together alone on a Pacific island."

Damion gave an exaggerated sigh. "Okay, I'll be right with you." He brushed his finger down Lynn's cheek. "You know how I'm always at the mercy of my public, honey. I'm afraid duty calls. It's a bore, but don't go away because I'll be right back as soon as I can. Lionel's arranged dancing in the other room, and I'm definitely planning to dance with you."

"I'll look forward to that," she said, almost dizzy with happiness. Damion was going to dance with her! He was reluctant to leave her! In her most optimistic moments, she had never allowed herself to believe Adam's plan would be such an immediate and overwhelming success.

"I'll be waiting for you, Damion," she breathed

huskily, feeling as if she were floating somewhere near the twelve-foot high ceiling. "Please, don't be too long."

She scarcely heard Adam's derisive snort as Damion took her hand and pressed a kiss against her fingertips, and she was only vaguely aware of his hand beneath her elbow as he guided her from the main reception room. She was startled when she returned to reality and found herself in the small room that had been set aside for dancing.

"What are we doing here?" she asked blankly. She had to shout her question because a five-piece rock band was belting out the latest hit song at a deafening noise level.

"We're going to dance," Adam shouted back.

"But Damion's already asked me to dance. Your plan's a success, Adam! Besides, he's not even in here at the moment. Surely there's no need to carry on with our charade any longer."

Adam's mouth tautened, and she heard impatience in his voice even through the din of the music. "Lynn, you're twenty-six years old, you work in the entertainment business, and you live in Manhattan. I can't believe you're still so naive. Damion casually suggested having a dance with you. That certainly doesn't constitute the beginning of a lifelong commitment. It doesn't even guarantee the start of a brief affair. Can't you see that Damion's the sort of man who's most interested in a woman if he has to chase after her? It's the thrill of the hunt that appeals to him, not its successful conclusion. I doubt if he knows what to do with his prey once he's captured it."

"You haven't seen him dealing with a mob of over-excited fans the way I have. It's no wonder he's tired of women throwing themselves at his feet."

"I didn't know it was his feet they were aiming

for," Adam muttered. "Anyway, whatever the reason for his attitude, you'll have a much greater chance for success if you're on the dance floor when he comes looking for you. What's the big deal, anyway? We've been dancing together since you were in high school. You have to do something to fill in the time while Damion's being photographed."

Everything he said was perfectly true, so she didn't resist when he led her out onto the small parquet floor. She danced well, a whole heap better than she acted, she thought ruefully, and she soon lost herself in the pulsating beat of the music. She was laughing, Damion momentarily forgotten, when the lights dimmed and the music slowed. The lead singer turned the amplifiers down several decibels and began to croon the words of a popular ballad. He actually had quite a good voice, Lynn thought dreamily.

Adam pulled her close, and her body flowed against his with the familiarity engendered by their years of friendship. Except that tonight the familiarity seemed subtly altered, and she felt none of the warm comfort she usually experienced in his arms. Her hands were trapped against the starched front of his evening shirt, so that she felt only crisp linen beneath her fingers, while his hands moved languorously on the bare skin of her back, somehow making her extraordinarily aware of the intimacy of his touch and the skimpiness of her dress. She tried to put some distance between herself and Adam, but his hands slid to her hips, pressing her so close that she couldn't avoid feeling his thighs moving against her. After only a few moments, her knees began to quiver.

And that was the difference between tonight and all the other nights, she realized suddenly. Before, whenever she had danced with Adam, he had held her impersonally, careful to preserve a discreet distance between their bodies. Tonight he was holding her as if he desired her, and the movement of his hands seemed deliberately erotic. Most confusing of all, she was having to fight the impulse to respond. Her head felt heavy, and after struggling for a while to hold it upright, she allowed it to drop forward and rest against Adam's chest.

Just for an instant his steps faltered, and they lost the rhythm of the dance. He murmured an apology and simultaneously stopped the slow stroking of his hands along her spine.

"Damion came in five minutes ago," he said quietly.

"Oh." For a moment she couldn't think of anything else to say. It was disconcerting to realize that she hadn't noticed Damion's arrival. It was even more disconcerting to realize that the sexual tension she had felt building between herself and Adam had been entirely a product of her own imagination. He had obviously been stroking her back to impress Damion, not because he couldn't resist the feel of her skin beneath his fingertips. She moistened her dry lips.

"Is Damion already dancing?" she asked after a minute or two.

"Yes. He's with Tiffany Brandon, but he's looking in this direction."

She was still uncomfortably aware of the tight thread of tension that seemed to stretch between them. It distracted her, making it difficult to concentrate on Damion's presence in the room. "Perhaps we should sit out the rest of this dance," she suggested.

"On the contrary," he said softly, "I think we should provide Damion with something worth looking at."

There was no time for her to react to his words. His mouth descended far more swiftly than she could turn her head away, and he took her lips in a kiss that was hard, expert, and unexpectedly hungry.

She closed her eyes, telling herself that shock caused the sharp arrow of desire to angle through her body. Only the knowledge that the darkened room was crowded with people prevented her from abandoning herself completely to the domination of his kiss.

The singer ended the ballad, and the lights gradually began to come on again. Adam dropped his arms and moved slightly away from her. "I would apologize," he said, "but Damion's walking toward us right this minute, so from your point of view I guess that makes everything worthwhile."

Damion tapped her on the shoulder before she could reply.

"Lynn, honey, I've come to claim my dance." His gaze roamed sensually over her body, then he turned and gave Adam one of his famous smiles. "I know you'll excuse us. I've been wanting to talk to my office manager all night."

"Certainly," Adam replied, smiling with equal politeness. "Lynn told me she had to attend the party tonight strictly for business reasons." Despite his superficial courtesy, the look he gave Lynn was enigmatic. "Have fun, Lynn," he said, and walked quickly from the dance floor.

This was the moment she had been waiting for, Lynn thought as Damion folded her tightly into his arms. Her heart didn't beat any faster when he lifted her hands and clasped them around his neck, but it was already beating so fast that it probably wasn't capable of increasing its speed. He whirled her masterfully in the direction of the musicians and murmured something to the lead singer. The band immediately broke into the pulsating theme music from the latest dance movie.

Damion was well over six feet tall, but he was a superb dancer, agile on his feet and calculatedly sensuous in his gestures. It was exhilarating to dance with him, and the floor soon cleared of other couples as an admiring audience gathered around to watch their exuberant partnership. Lynn forgot the strange tensions of the evening as Damion called forth every ounce of her dancing ability in a series of flashy, demanding movements. Their exhibition culminated in a sweeping turn that left her collapsed over Damion's arm, her head thrown back, her throat stylishly vulnerable to his embrace.

He was far too much the professional performer to actually kiss her, of course, which for some odd reason was something of a relief. He leaned over her, beaming as he pulled her upright, acknowledging the applause from their audience with a deprecatory wave of his hand. She looked around for Adam, feeling a curious moment of blankness when she glimpsed his blond head bent close to Tiffany Brandon's cascading brown ringlets.

The other dancers began to drift back onto the floor. Lynn's cheeks were already burning with heat. She knew they must have flamed even brighter when Damion lifted her hand to his mouth and dropped a moist kiss on her palm.

"You were absolutely terrific, Lynn, honey. Where've you been hiding yourself all this time? I had no idea you could dance like that."

"You never asked me," she said, then bit her lip, appalled that she sounded so grouchy. "It was wonderful dancing with somebody who's as talented as you are, Damion."

He laughed with boyish modesty and dropped another kiss into her palm. "Lynn, babe, let's go get a drink, and then we'll dance again. I haven't enjoyed myself so much in weeks."

They danced together twice more, until the irate

publicity agent came to haul Damion away. "Dammit, Lynn, what's gotten into you?" he said, scowling furiously. "You should know better than to monopolize Damion's time like this. Tiffany's waiting, and she's madder than a pregnant hornet."

Ignoring his agent, Damion took both of Lynn's hands and raised them to his lips, his marvelous blue eyes glancing at her through thick, black lashes. It was a wonderfully romantic gesture, one she had often seen him use to devastating effect on his TV show. "I guess we have to say good night, Lynn, honey," he said regretfully. "I'll see you tomorrow morning."

"Yes, I'll be there at eight. There's a lot of correspondence waiting for your signature, and don't forget you have a telephone consultation scheduled with Bruce Adams for nine-thirty."

"I won't forget, babe. Not with you and Betty there to remind me." Damion squeezed her hands casually, then walked off with his harried publicity agent. Lynn kicked herself mentally. Why on earth had she introduced that prosaic note of business into their farewell? She had totally destroyed the romantic mood of their parting. Feeling curiously flat, she wandered out into the hallway where she found Adam lounging by the only window, smoking a cigarette.

Her eyes widened in astonishment. "I didn't know you smoked, Adam."

He crushed the butt out in an overflowing ashtray, and she wondered if all those stubs could possibly be his. "I don't usually," he said curtly. He straightened, and she was surprised to detect signs of intense fatigue in the taut line of his mouth. "How do you rate your evening with Damion?" he asked, his voice level. "From what I could see, it seemed an overwhelming success."

"It was fine, I guess. That is, it was more than

fine. It was terrific. He would have danced with me some more if only his publicity agent hadn't come and taken him away. Damion told me he hadn't had so much fun with anybody in weeks."

"Wonderful." Adam stared out of the darkened window. "Are you ready to leave? I have an early start tomorrow morning, and it's getting late."

"Yes, we can leave now." She touched him lightly on the arm, and he finally turned to look at her.

"Yes?"

"I just wanted to say thank you, Adam. For tonight. For everything. You're a good friend."

A reflected beam of light from the overhead fixture gave his eyes an unnaturally hard brilliance. "Don't mention it," he said, and his smile contained a definite twist of mockery. "It's been my pleasure, Lynn, *babe*."

CHAPTER FIVE

THE MINUTE DAMION and Lynn were alone in his private office the next day, he seized the opportunity to invite her out to dinner. She nearly cheered out loud at this further proof of how successful Adam's plan was proving. Mindful of Adam's parting instructions, however, she fought back her excitement and managed to resist the urge to accept Damion's invitation.

"I'm awfully sorry," she said, her heart in her mouth in case he didn't renew his invitation. "I'd love to go out with you, but I already have a date for dinner tonight."

"With that man... with Adam Hunter?" he asked.

"Um, yes. Yes, with Adam."

"What is he to you, Lynn?"

"He's a very old friend," she said, blushing. Although she had told the exact truth, she knew her answer sounded like a lie. "We've known each other forever," she added. "Our parents are friends."

"If you can't have dinner, would you have lunch with me?" Damion asked.

A small thrill of gratification tingled down her spine, and she abandoned any lingering idea of playing hard to get. "Thank you," she said. "I'd really like that."

"You're looking fabulous again today, Lynn. Like a different person. I can't believe the change in you these last couple of days. That blouse is new, isn't it?"

"Yes, it is." She touched the soft, pale lilac folds. "I'm glad you like it, Damion."

"It's the person inside that I really like. You're a wonderful woman, Lynn. I'm only now beginning to realize just how wonderful. Good to look at and more than competent at your job."

He took her hand and started to raise it to his lips. When he saw that she was holding a bundle of pencils, he stopped in mid-lift and patted her knuckles. "I'll be counting the minutes until lunchtime, babe."

"Shall I make a reservation for us, Damion?"

"I'll do it." His voice lowered to a husky whisper. "I want to surprise you with my choice."

Lynn floated out of his private office and plopped down at her desk, staring dreamily at the typewriter keys until a question from Betty brought her back to reality. She completed her routine office chores in a euphoric haze, her thought processes not really operating normally until Betty said good-bye when she left to buy a grapefruit for lunch.

Damion was busy with a long-distance call, so with the office empty, she decided to use one of the other lines to call Adam. She had promised to keep him informed on how things progressed.

"Hello, Lynn, how are you this morning?" he asked, when she'd finally penetrated his screen of assistants.

"Everything's working out just like you said it would!" she replied excitedly, without preamble. "Damion asked me out to dinner tonight, but I took your advice about playing hard to get, and I told him I had a date with you. So he asked me out to lunch instead. We'll be leaving any minute. Isn't it great?"

"Terrific. I'm very happy for you." There was an infinitesimal pause. "What time would you like me to pick you up tonight? I can make any time after seven-thirty."

"Pick me up?"

"For dinner. You told Damion you have a date with me. Fortunately I'm free tonight, so I'll be able to help you keep up appearances."

"Oh, I see. Well, I guess eight o'clock would be good for me."

"I'll look forward to hearing all about your lunch date. You can tell me everything Damion says, and we'll plot the next stage of our strategy."

It was only after she had hung up that she suddenly stopped to wonder who they were keeping up appearances for. After all, Damion never called her apartment or came to visit, so he wasn't going to know whether or not she actually went out with Adam. But she had no time to pursue the thought because at that moment Damion finished his phone call and came into her office.

"Ready, babe?" His blue eyes shot her a glance laden with meaning, and her bones felt as if they were starting to melt. "I've made a reservation in the Rainbow Room."

The restaurant was located almost at the top of Rockefeller Center. He took all the women he most enjoyed dating there, and Lynn glowed with pleasure to think that he had chosen to take her there, too. He couldn't have indicated more clearly that he was changing the basis of their relationship from something strictly professional to something much more personal.

His hands lingered on her shoulders as he helped her into her jacket, and she still glowed with inner warmth when the elevator arrived in the lobby. During the cab ride they talked about the opening of Damion's new play, which was scheduled to take place at the beginning of November. He asked her opinion of certain crucial scenes in the second act, and she gave a great deal of thought to her answers, sensing his need to discuss his interpretation with somebody who had professional expertise but who was not involved with the actual production. It was this sort of discussion that had fascinated her from the very beginning of her work for him, and caught up in their exchange of technical opinions, she was oblivious to their progress downtown. She was surprised when the cab pulled up at their destination, seemingly only a few minutes after they got into it.

Lynn had never been to the Rainbow Room, since the prices were far beyond the scope of her budget, and she found the famous view from the restaurant's wide windows as spectacular as she had heard it to be.

A short silence fell after the waiter had settled them at their secluded corner table. "Central Park looks lovely from here," she commented as she opened the menu. "The sun shining on all those yellow leaves is really beautiful."

"Yes, New York looks good at the moment, but the leaves will all vanish at the first windstorm, and then we'll have months of winter to get through. I loathe New York in winter."

"We had a terrible time last year, didn't we? All that snow. I hope it's better this year."

She couldn't believe the course of their conversation. She had never imagined that she would waste her first date with Damion talking about the vagaries of New York's weather. Another short silence fell while they examined the menu. Damion recommended the grilled Dover sole, and Lynn agreed, preferring to eat something reasonably light. The waiter took their orders and brought glasses of iced club soda, garnished with thin slices of lime. Lynn sipped hers gratefully. She was finding it absurdly difficult to think of anything to say.

Fortunately Damion took charge of the conversation. "The sun streaming through the window is giving your hair a deep russet glow," he said, reaching across the table to take her fingers into his clasp.

"Is it? I always think of my hair as brown, but it was quite blond when I was a child. Actually, my mother had auburn hair when she got married, although it's all gray now, of course."

Lynn finally managed to clamp her lips shut. My God, she thought, from the weather to her mother. How was that for sparkling conversation with the man she'd been dying to go out with for nearly ten months?

Damion chose not to pursue the topic of Mrs. Frampton's original hair color. He stroked his fingers along Lynn's forearm. "Feel how cold I am," he said huskily. "Feel how warm you are. I want to warm myself in your fire, Lynn, babe."

His throaty voice imparted a heart-stopping sensuality to the remark, but its effect was somewhat lost on Lynn since she'd already heard it in the final episode of last season's TV series.

"Actually, I'm a bit cold myself," she said, withdrawing her hand from his and taking another sip of club soda. She spotted their waiter crossing the room and smiled brightly. "Look, here comes our food. I'm hungry, aren't you?"

"I'm not hungry for fish," he said. He paused, waiting for her to say something, but when she made no response he lowered his voice dramatically. "I'm only hungry for you, Lynn."

She gulped. "The sole looks very appetizing, Damion. I think you should try it first."

The remark sounded so ludicrous that she had to bite back a gurgle of laughter. Damion's magnificent eyebrows drew together in a faint frown, and she added hastily, "Tell me what you've decided to do about that movie offer. You know, Damion, you never told me the final outcome of all those discussions with your agent."

His frown vanished with miraculous swiftness, and he launched into an enthusiastic monologue about his decision to accept the movie role and his intention to move to Hollywood for the duration of the filming. Financial backing for the movie had already been obtained.

"My name was enough to secure the funds," he said. "Once they knew I'd agreed to play the part, financing was a breeze."

"That's good, Damion."

He returned to his elaboration of the career opportunities his move to Hollywood would open up, and when the waiter had filled their coffee cups, he looked at Lynn earnestly. "I'm counting on you," he said. "You will move to California with me, won't you? I don't know what I'd do without you around to manage my office, Lynn."

For some reason the invitation did not completely thrill her, but she said, "Of course, I'd love to come with you, Damion. If I can work out the practical details. There's my family to think of and my apartment and—"

"But you'd be working with me, Lynn, and that's the important thing. If you stay in New York, I'll hardly ever be around, at least for the six months it takes to finish the movie."

"I'm flattered that you should ask me, Damion. Of course I am. In fact I'm thrilled."

"Then it's all settled. You can fly out there as soon as we've got this play opening out of the way, and you can start looking around for suitable office space. Maybe in a couple of weeks I can take a few days off myself." His blue eyes gazed burningly into hers. "We'll fly out together, honey, and you can help me choose my house. Something in Malibu, I think, right on the ocean."

She decided that the knot in her stomach had to be caused by excitement. She swallowed hard, finding her mouth suddenly dry.

"That would be lovely, Damion," she said in a small voice. "I'll certainly look forward to our trip."

That evening, when Lynn started to stroke mauve eyeshadow across her lids, her hand suddenly stopped in mid-movement. She stared silently into the mirror, then grabbed a wad of tissue and began to rub fiercely at the layers of tinted foundation, blusher, and lip gloss. She splashed great scoops of water onto her face, then stared again at her reflection. Even without the campaign warpaint, she didn't look quite the same as she had a week earlier. Her eyes held a trace of self-awareness combined with a hint of wariness that was entirely new.

"You look about ten years more sophisticated than you did last week," she told her reflection, then shrugged, impatient with herself and annoyed that she had wiped off her makeup. She had no intention of reverting to her former, clean-scrubbed image, so she would simply have to start all over again. And she wasn't even sure what she'd been trying to prove in the first place. Damion Tanner was a first-rate actor and a nationwide television star. Once his movie was finished, he would probably be recognized as a successful actor all over the world. And this famous, talented man had invited her out to dinner. At lunchtime he had virtually told her that he desired her. It was a situation guaranteed to boost any woman's ego, so naturally she looked more self-aware. She hadn't needed to moon over her image in the bathroom mirror to discover that great truth.

Glancing at her wristwatch, she realized it was already eight o'clock, and Adam was nearly always punctual. She quickly reapplied blusher, lip gloss, eye shadow, and a touch of mascara, hearing the intercom buzz just as she was running a comb through her hair. She depressed the button on the speaker and told Adam to come on up, thrusting her feet into a pair of high-heeled sandals while she was talking.

A few moments later she opened the door to a lean, blond, tanned stranger. She blinked, and the unfamiliar image wavered, then returned to the Adam Hunter she had known and been friends with for years.

"Ready to leave?" he asked, smiling.

She turned away from him. "Would you come in and have a drink first?"

She heard him close her front door and follow her into the living room. "What is it, Lynn?" he asked quietly.

She poured out a small amount of Scotch, adding several ice cubes before turning to hand it to him.

"Thanks," he said. He waited for her to say something, but when she remained silent he sat down on the sofa, relaxing comfortably against the cushions. "Do you want to tell me what's bothering you, Lynn? I'm happy to offer my best-quality advice if you'd like to hear it. On the other hand, we don't have to talk about it, if you'd prefer not to."

The confession unexpectedly burst out of her. "Nothing's bothering me, except that I think maybe I'm going crazy." She smiled nervously, trying to make a joke out of her words and failing abysmally.

"You seem pretty sane to me," he said, matching her pretense of lightness. "You've never told me that you're the Empress of Russia, and I've never once caught you talking to a lamppost."

"But if you'd arrived five minutes earlier, you'd have caught me talking to my mirror." She locked her hands tightly together. "Adam, I'm beginning to wonder if ten months of secret passion for Damion Tanner has warped my brain."

"I've heard that those secret passions will do it to you every time," he said.

She smiled, but it vanished quickly. "It's not only my feelings for Damion," she said. "It's you, Adam. You've been my best friend for years now. I've always felt as if I knew everything about you, even what you were thinking, because we were so close. Do you know that the last three times we've met, there were actually a few seconds when I didn't recognize you? Is that crazy or what?"

"Not crazy. Interesting."

Something in his voice touched off a shiver deep inside her, and she whirled around in a fury of frustration. "And that's another thing. Half the time recently you'll say something, and I'll suspect you of having some deep, hidden meaning. Haven't you noticed what's happening to us, Adam? I jump every time you come within a foot of me. You're one of the most important people in my life, and I can't stand this weird sense of strain between us. Something's happened to you, Adam, it must have. Has California changed you or something? Have you dyed your hair or had plastic surgery on your nose? Why do I keep getting this sensation of looking at a stranger? Why do you seem so . . . different?"

He took a sip of his whiskey, then stirred the ice with his forefinger. "I haven't dyed my hair, and I haven't had plastic surgery. Apart from the tan, I guess I look pretty much the way I've always looked." He glanced up. "I don't think any very significant changes have occurred in my life recently, Lynn. And I'm sure I'm behaving toward you pretty much as I've always behaved toward you."

"That can't be true. I never used to jump when you touched me. In fact, I never even used to notice, and yet you must have touched me a hundred times—a thousand times—since we first knew one another."

"Yes, your reactions certainly seem a little more sensitive recently."

"Why?" she asked bluntly. "What's happened?"

"You've changed," he said.

"Adam, please don't be cryptic. I'm confused enough without having to cope with your obscure comments."

"I didn't intend to sound mysterious. I only meant that you've changed in the past few months, and so maybe your perception of me has changed, too."

"That can't be, Adam. I know you too well."

"I sometimes think you hardly know me at all."

"Dammit, you're being cryptic again!"

He laughed, and the look he gave her was very direct, but his gray eyes provided no clue to his real feelings. How had she ever looked at that opaque, silvery screen and thought that Adam was easy to understand?

He spoke softly when he answered her. "There are some things, Lynn, that I can't tell you. You have to work them out for yourself."

She pushed her hand distractedly through her hair. "All this started when I told you how I felt about Damion. Is that it? I *knew* I should never have agreed to that insane suggestion of yours about pretending to be in love with me. Is this crazy charade messing things up for us?"

He took a final swallow of his whiskey. "I hope not," he said, getting to his feet in a lithe, easy movement. "I thought the campaign was proving a stunning success. Damion asked you out to lunch today. Undoubtedly he'll ask you for another date tomorrow. Nothing's messed up, is it? Damion's intrigued by you, and I thought that was what the charade was all about."

"I guess so," she said unhappily, carrying his empty glass out to the kitchen.

He propped himself against the kitchen counter, watching while she removed her coat from the closet. "If you think about it rationally, Lynn, there's no way your relationship with Damion could affect our relationship. After all, you want him as a lover, and you want me as a friend. Those are two entirely different roles, and I don't see how one could be confused with the other. Do you?"

"No. No, I guess not."

He made no comment on the lingering uncertainty in her voice. He reached out and adjusted the back of her coat collar, then handed her a pair of gloves from the closet shelf. "I've made reservations at the restaurant for eight-thirty, and they'll give our table away if we're late. Shall we go?"

He took her to a quiet restaurant on Third Avenue that specialized in Hungarian food. They ordered the recommended specialty of the house, breast of chicken cooked in butter and paprika, then settled back to enjoy a glass of dry white wine. Gradually Lynn felt herself relax.

"So how was your lunch date?" Adam asked eventually. "I've been looking forward to hearing everything that happened."

"It was fine." For some reason she didn't much want to talk about her lunch date. She swirled the wine around in the glass. "Damion's going to spend six months on the West Coast making a movie. He's asked me to go with him."

The crust of the crisp French bread Adam was holding crumbled between his fingers. He reached for his napkin before answering her. "And are you going?" he asked finally.

"I haven't decided yet. What's it like in California, Adam? I've never been there, you know."

He didn't ask why her reaction to Damion's invitation was so wishy-washy, which was a great relief since she had no idea what her answer would be. For a woman who had always considered herself very aware of her own motivations, she seemed suddenly to be totally incapable of deciding what she really wanted.

Fortunately Adam took her question at face value and gave her a brief, entertaining description of the various California regions. The waiter brought their platters of chicken very quickly and instructed them to enjoy their dinners. She spoke as soon as he left the table.

"I've never really understood exactly what you were doing out in California these past few months, Adam.

You've been flying out there so frequently for the last couple of years. Could you tell me something about your work?"

"That sounds like an opening line straight out of *Emily Post's Guide to Initiating Conversation with an Unfamiliar Gentleman.*"

She laughed. "If I sounded stilted, it was because I suddenly realized that I've never asked you about your work in California. It was an embarrassing realization."

She felt heat creep up and flame scarlet in her cheeks. "In fact, when I think about it, we've only talked about the topics that interest me when we've been together. We must have spent hours discussing the New York entertainment industry and my plans for the future, yet until last weekend I never even knew that you'd branched out of financial consulting and into property development."

"I can't cope with you when you're in such a penitential mood. It's definitely out of character. Would you like a signed statement from me admitting that I've always avoided talking about my work when I was with you?"

"No. I just want you to tell me more about what you've been doing out in California. I'm truly interested, Adam."

He didn't tease her any longer. Instead he explained concisely about the land he had bought and the shopping center he had developed in an area previously remote from major stores and supermarkets. The area, called Avon Hills, had experienced a massive population growth five years previously, and the local residents had badly needed adequate shopping facilities.

The town was built on a hillside and was exceptionally beautiful. It was also extremely difficult to develop further. The major problem had been bringing together architects, shop owners, and town planners who were prepared to pay the extra money needed to erect a plaza that was both efficient and environmentally safe as well as aesthetically pleasing. Adam downplayed the importance of his own contribution, but reading between the lines, Lynn concluded that the project would never have been brought to a successful conclusion without his financial expertise and considerable powers of persuasion.

"Are you going to become involved in more large-scale property developments in California?" she asked. "Or was Avon Hills a one-time endeavor?"

"I'm interested in doing more development projects," he replied. "I still do a little financial consulting for my old clients, but over the last two years my company has moved more and more into land development and investment in urban rehabilitation projects. For quite a few years after World War II, builders bought up tracts of land and developed communities as if land, water, and trees were endless commodities, perpetually available. Now everybody's screaming because they've discovered that communities can run out of water, that trees can die from pollution, and that the land has often been devastated by irresponsible development techniques. I want to show that it's possible to build communities that are financially sound investments and yet environmentally conservative. I want to convince people that the most beautiful solution is often the most practical solution, provided that the financing is properly worked out. I hope to continue with projects in both California and the New York area, because those are two of the regions that have the most challenging problems. Of course, they have the most exciting opportunities as well."

"Are you planning to buy an apartment in California?" Lynn asked.

"I haven't decided," he said. "Obviously, I'm going to be doing quite a bit of traveling over the next few years wherever I buy housing."

"Well, at least if I move out to L.A. we'll still be able to see each other quite often."

"Yes, I suppose we will." The waiter removed their dinner plates, and they ordered chilled fruit and two glasses of the sweet Tokay dessert wine that Hungary was famous for.

"What about you, Lynn?" he asked as they sipped the slightly thick, golden wine. "Have you ever thought about changing the direction of your career? With your administrative skills and your flair for personnel management, you're not limited to working in a small office."

"You're forgetting that I worked at the East Side Theatrical Agency before Damion recruited me. That's one of the biggest agencies in town, nearly thirty people on the staff, and I didn't enjoy it all that much. I think maybe I'm better suited to a smaller, more personal office."

"There are other organizations in the world apart from theatrical agencies, you know. You've always hungered for a career associated with the performing arts, but are you sure that's what you really want to do in the long term?"

"It's where my skills are strongest."

"I think you're wrong, Lynn," he said quietly. "You have a supple body, and you've always been an outstanding dancer, but you were smart enough to recognize years ago that you aren't quite good enough to cut it as a professional."

"But I was never really interested in dancing. Acting and the theater most fascinate me. They always have."

"True, you had great fun performing in high school

plays, and I'm sure you'll always enjoy going to the theater or seeing a good movie. But I don't think acting's your real talent any more than dancing is. You know, Lynn, you have a flair for organization and administration that goes beyond mere efficiency."

She smiled ruefully. "Now there's a talent calculated to set people's pulses racing."

"Believe me, it's a talent calculated to make any business executive's heart positively gallop with excitement. If you only knew how much difficulty I had recruiting competent people to run Avon Hills, you'd realize how much your organizational abilities are in demand."

"I've never considered working outside the entertainment industry," she said slowly. "I love being involved with television and the theater, even if it's only on the periphery. I find my work with Damion very satisfying, Adam."

"I'm sure you do. I just wanted to point out that you have several options open to you. Your choice isn't limited to going to California with Damion or looking for another job in the entertainment industry."

The waiter returned to the table to pour their coffee, and the conversation shifted to an old house in the far western corner of Connecticut that they had visited together last summer. It was still on the market, and Adam had vague plans to buy and renovate it as a summer home. They discussed the practical advantages of the idea—which were few—and the potential pleasures, which seemed likely to be high. Then their conversation drifted easily into an exchange of opinions about a new biography of Abraham Lincoln they had both read recently.

When they finally emerged into the cool night, they walked a few blocks looking for a cab. Lynn reflected that, although the food had been delicious, she had hardly noticed the progression of the meal because she and Adam had been so busy talking. She mentally contrasted the easy flow of their conversation tonight with the awkward silences of her luncheon date with Damion. She had a suspicion that the gaps at lunch-time had occurred because she and Damion had nothing much in common except their mutual interest in his career. It was an uncomfortable thought for somebody who had believed herself madly in love less than twenty-four hours earlier.

When the cab drew up outside Lynn's apartment, Adam asked the driver to wait. He escorted Lynn into her building, waiting while she summoned the elevator.

"Thank you for a lovely evening," she said. "It was great fun."

"Thank you for joining me." He tipped up her chin and dropped a casual kiss on the end of her nose. "Call me next time you need to impress Damion, and I'll be happy to escort you again. I'm beginning to enjoy these dates of ours. We haven't spent so much time alone together in years."

"I don't expect I'll have to impose on you any more, Adam. I think Damion is quite likely to ask me out again, so we don't need to keep trying to spark his interest." She knew her smile was stiff, but she couldn't help it. "Your plan was a big success."

His eyes gleamed with sudden humor. "Not yet, Lynn, but I think it's getting there."

Her elevator arrived, and she stepped into it. The electronic doors whooshed shut, blocking him from her view.

By the time she reached her apartment she was almost convinced that she hadn't wanted him to kiss her.

CHAPTER SIX

TIFFANY BRANDON ARRIVED unexpectedly in the office at ten the next morning and insisted on speaking to Damion. She left again ten minutes later, ignoring Lynn and Betty and slamming the door behind her as she flounced out.

Betty glanced across at Lynn, her eyebrows raised. "I guess that has to be one of the shortest affairs in Damion's record. As far as I could see, it never even got off the ground. Does he have another leading lady lined up that I don't know about?"

Lynn shuffled a few papers from one side of her desk to the other. "Damion's going to make a movie soon—you'll be seeing the contracts by the end of next week—but I don't know who the female lead is going to be. I'm not sure if it's even been decided."

At that moment Damion buzzed the intercom and

asked Lynn to come into his private office. When she entered, she found him sitting in his favorite chair by the window, a script open on his lap.

"Do you want to know why Tiffany was so angry?" he asked without preamble. "She's scheduled to attend the gala opening of some new movie tonight, and her publicity agent told her to take me with her. She's furious because I won't go." His mouth twisted. "It's ironic, you know, Lynn. In this profession we're all so damned busy using each other, we forget that there are still some people left in the world who go out together simply to enjoy themselves."

He tossed the script onto a table and stood up, his eyes losing their momentary bleakness. "There's another one of those darn studio parties tomorrow," he said. "Will you come with me? As my date, not as my office manager."

"To protect you from Tiffany's claws?"

He shook his head, grinning.

"Chiefly because I enjoy your company, although the protection against scratches would be an added bonus."

"Well, thank you. I'd like to come," she said, wondering even as she spoke if she was telling the exact truth. It was a realization not calculated to add to her peace of mind, which was already in a precarious state after a long and restless night.

They put in three hours of intensive work before Damion had to leave for a taping session, and the rest of the day continued at such a hectic pace that Lynn had very little chance to analyze her feelings about Damion's latest invitation. On the whole, she decided, it was probably just as well.

She had already agreed to eat dinner with Betty at her home in Long Island that evening. "I'm getting to be a whiz at broiling chicken breasts and making spinach salad," Betty had said when she issued the invitation. "And you can even have dressing on your salad, so it won't be a total sacrifice on your part. My husband and I will watch you and feel envious."

It was six o'clock before they could get away from the office, and after seven by the time they reached Betty's house. Betty's husband was already home, squeezing lemon juice over the chicken and expertly drying spinach leaves. Lynn had always thought it would be impossible to find anybody else as good-tempered as her secretary, but Harry's easygoing nature clearly equaled that of his wife, and everyone thoroughly enjoyed the dinner.

They were clearing the dishes from the table when three of Betty's grandchildren arrived for a visit.

"Hi, Gramps. Glad you're home, Gran." Their grandson reached into the refrigerator and helped himself to a giant glass of milk. "Dad threw us out of the house," he remarked cheerfully. "He said they'd be carrying him away in a white canvas jacket if we didn't get out and let him have a few minutes' peace and quiet. So we came to visit you."

"How nice of you," Betty said. "We're certainly flattered." The irony in her voice was totally lost on her grandchildren. She introduced the two girls and their elder brother to Lynn, and they responded politely before separating into three different rooms, where they set up three different tape recorders and played three different tunes, all at maximum volume. Betty's smile never faded, and despite the ear-shattering noise, her husband actually fell asleep in the armchair where he had taken a newspaper to read after dinner.

"One of my daughters lives way out in Wyoming,

and the other one's in New Jersey," Betty said, calmly pouring Lynn a cup of coffee as if the ceiling weren't shaking. "It's good to have Alison's children just around the corner."

Lynn accepted the coffee and glanced warily up to see if flakes of plaster had begun to fall. "I'm sure it must be," she murmured, but the rest of her words were drowned out in a crash of drums and cymbals.

She grinned, and Betty laughed openly. "I wish you could see your expression," she said. "Now you know why I love to come to work. It's better than a paid holiday."

"I understand why you like to work, but I can't imagine why you need to diet. I'd have thought the vibrations would shake off any excess fat cells before they had a chance to settle."

"It's my placid disposition that causes the trouble." Betty sighed. "Everybody else in our business works off their lunchtime calories producing ulcers. Mine sink straight to my hips. I've decided my weight problem is caused by the fact that I've never learned how to worry."

Later that night, as she stared at the illuminated dial of her alarm clock, Lynn wished she suffered from Betty's enviable problem. For the past week or so she seemed to have done nothing but worry. In the silence of her apartment several uncomfortable facts were rearing up and virtually demanding to be acknowledged. She squirmed deeper into bed, pulled the covers over her head, and refused to think about them.

It had taken her ten months of waiting, not to mention Adam's intervention, to get Damion to notice her. Now he was finally showing definite signs of finding her attractive. It was not the moment to start wondering what had originally caused her to fall in love . . . or if she had ever actually been in love with him at all.

Damion was out of the office all the next day, and by the time she rushed home to change for the party, she was almost too tired to feel anything. That had to be why she felt so little excitement at the prospect of spending an entire evening in his exhilarating company.

She dressed in an Edwardian-style, dusky pink gown with a high lace collar and tight cuffs. Pink satin ribbon and a furl of frothy beige lace decorated the hem of the ankle-length skirt. She had bought the dress to wear as maid-of-honor at a friend's wedding, but the wedding had been called off at the last minute, and she'd never worn the outfit. She was afraid it might be a bit too demure for a sophisticated Manhattan party, but she had no real choice.

She was fastening the last of the tiny pearl buttons on her sleeve when Damion arrived at her apartment.

"You look fabulous, sugar," he said as soon as she opened the door. His eyes glowed with admiration as he swiftly inspected her. "Seeing you dressed like that, I can understand why Victorian men used to go crazy at the sight of a woman's ankle. You're covered from head to toe, yet the dress is incredibly provocative. We're going to rock 'em back on their heels when we arrive together, babe."

"I'm glad you like it, Damion," she said woodenly.

His prophecy about their entrance proved entirely correct. When Lynn walked into the room on Damion's arm, the babble of party conversation died away to an ego-boosting silence. He waited until the eyes of virtually every guest were upon them, then lifted her hand to his lips in a courtly gesture very much in keeping with the old-fashioned style of her evening gown. Press bulbs flashed, then the hum of conversation gradually increased to its previous roar as guests crowded around them.

The party was much the same as the one she had attended three nights earlier, when Adam had been her escort. The guest list had been changed, but the cast members of the television series were all there, the professional publicity people were identical, and the band was playing exactly the same songs. Logs blazed once again in the black marble fireplace, and the food looked indistinguishable from the previous occasion. It was being ignored just as it had been on Monday, and once again the bartenders were having a hectic time.

Even Tiffany Brandon was there, looking stunning in a sequined gown that had no back and almost no front. Her famous bosom was visibly proven to be entirely her own. She went very well with the young Adonis who was her escort, Lynn decided. She looked as if she would pop out of her dress; he looked as if he had been sewn into his trousers. She wondered what would happen if either of them ever needed to sit down.

Damion was kept talking by one reporter after another. Lynn smiled a great deal and fielded questions with the expertise she had acquired during the past ten months. After the first hour, her mind began to wander. A major critic for *The New York Times* came up and asked Damion a penetrating question about his forthcoming play. The public relations agency, Lynn thought absently, was really doing an outstanding job of getting the right people here tonight. When she got back to the office tomorrow, she would have to remember to call and congratulate them.

Suddenly aware that she had a splitting headache, she wished she could get a drink of water. She hadn't eaten lunch, she remembered, and there hadn't been time for dinner. Maybe she should try some of the caterer's canapés. On the other hand, she might discover they were made of plastic instead of real food. Perhaps that was why nobody ever ate them. The absurd thought made her smile, and she glanced up to discover both Damion and the reporter looking at her expectantly.

She had to ask the reporter to repeat his question, and after that she tried harder to prevent her attention from drifting away. Eventually Damion escorted her into the other room and led her out onto the dance floor. At his smiling request the band broke into an old-fashioned waltz, and soon, as it had before, an admiring audience gathered around them. Thunderous applause greeted their final, spectacular twirl.

They danced a while longer, then Damion pulled her close. "Let's get out of here, babe, and go back to my apartment. I want to be alone with you."

There was absolutely no doubt that the sudden knot in her stomach was caused by nervous uncertainty, not by breathless anticipation. Lynn looked up into the burning blue eyes of the man who had obsessed her for ten months and told herself she must be mistaken. Perhaps she was too tired to recognize her own feelings. She had been yearning for this moment for weeks. Surely at any minute her knees would start to quiver, just as they did when Adam held her . . . She clamped off the treacherous thought, not wanting to deal with it and stared again into the depths of Damion's eyes. She had never even kissed him, she reminded herself. How could she know what her true feelings were if she had never tested them?

She thought quickly. In her own apartment she would have more control over the situation. "Why don't you come back to my place?" she heard herself say. The words sounded hollow, as if they had traveled from a great distance. She smiled, trying to cover up her doubts about the wisdom of the invitation. "I guarantee to make you the best Irish coffee you've ever tasted."

"Sounds fabulous," he whispered, the words husky with promise. "I'll tell my driver to bring the car around while you get your coat."

Damion made no attempt to hold her during the short drive home, but as soon as she closed the front door of her apartment, he slid her evening coat from her shoulders and pulled her back against his chest.

"Alone at last," he breathed.

She smiled, then realized he hadn't been joking when he uttered the tired cliché.

"So we are," she said brightly. She slid out of his arms and scurried into the tiny kitchen. "Um . . . why don't you relax on the sofa, Damion, while I fix the coffee?"

He flicked his famous lock of hair away from his famous eyebrow. "I'd rather watch you," he said throatily. "You have such dainty hands, Lynn. So competent looking, but so exquisitely feminine."

She felt him move up behind her, and her competent but exquisitely feminine hands immediately dropped the canister they were holding. Unground coffee beans spilled all over the counter and bounced across the floor. Damion watched them roll around his feet in pained disapproval, making no effort to catch any of them.

"I'm sorry," she said, biting her lip to contain a bubble of inappropriate laughter. "That was really clumsy of me."

"No matter," he said soothingly. "There's no need to apologize. I understand why you're nervous, Lynn, but there's really no reason to be."

Unfortunately she could think of dozens of reasons—more by the minute. "I'm afraid I'll have to ask you to get out of the kitchen, Damion," she said. "My dustpan is in that cupboard behind you, and I need to sweep up this mess before I make the coffee."

Damion gazed poignantly into her eyes, his features arranging themselves into the sensual expression that the cameras always captured for the final closeup of his television show. "There's no reason to sweep up now, honey." His voice lowered to a passionate murmur. "Who needs coffee, anyway?"

"Oh, I do, Damion!" she squeaked hastily. She cleared her throat and inched her arm away from his stroking fingers. "I absolutely, positively can't function without coffee. Haven't you noticed that Betty and I have a pot brewing in the office all the time?"

He placed his finger firmly on her lips. "Hush, babe, and I'll prove to you just how well you can function without coffee. Why would you need coffee when you have me around?"

He'd started to remove his dinner jacket while he was still speaking. She gulped as he tossed it carelessly onto a chair in her dining alcove and reached for his black bow tie, pulling it undone with a single practiced movement. His hands started to work expertly on the buttons of his starched evening shirt.

"Wait!" Lynn exclaimed frantically as the third button popped open. "You can't do that now, Damion! You can't get undressed!"

He laughed and removed his cuff links. "Why on earth not, sugar?"

"I'm—um—I'm expecting an important phone call from my parents. Yes, that's it! They'll be calling at any minute."

He turned around, saw the phone hanging on the

kitchen wall, and silently took it off the hook.

"Does that take care of the problem, honey?" He moved purposefully toward her, and she ducked under his outstretched arms, skidding on the spilled coffee beans as she hurried toward the relative safety of the center of her living room.

Damion followed her, and she stepped back as he approached. When the back of her knees touched the sofa, she drew in a deep breath and held out her hands to ward him off.

"Damion, I'm sorry," she said. "I should never have invited you to my apartment. I apologize if I've given you the wrong impression. You're a wonderful actor, and I admire you very much. In fact, I envy your talent. But I don't want to go to bed with you. Not tonight. Not ever."

He laughed easily. "Honey, you're so sweet, but there's no need to play hard to get. I want you, babe. You don't have to worry about making yourself seem interesting."

"That's really not what I'm trying to do, Damion. I'm not playing hard to get. I'm not playing any game at all. I'm truly flattered that you want to go to bed with me, but the fact is, I'm sure it wouldn't be a success. We work so well together. Let's not spoil a terrific relationship by trying to turn it into something it's not."

She might as well not have spoken for all the effect she had on him.

"I adore shy women," he said as he once again moved purposefully toward her.

"I am *not* shy," she retorted as she ducked under his arms and ran around the coffee table. "Damion, for heaven's sake, I don't want to go to bed with you!"

She felt a brief urge to giggle at the thought of how

absurd they must look, dodging each other around the furniture. But the situation was potentially not at all amusing. She doubted if any woman had refused Damion's advances in years, and she had no idea how he would react when he discovered that she was deadly serious in her refusals.

He caught up with her on the second swing around the living room and took her into his arms. "Lynn, babe, let's stop playing games now. Which way is the bedroom?"

"There isn't one. I sleep on the sofa. I mean, the sofa turns into a bed." She knew she was babbling, but she couldn't stop. "It's very comfortable actually. I don't really need a separate bedroom."

"Well then, what are we waiting for, babe?"

What indeed? "Oh, heavens, I forgot," she exclaimed, desperation endowing her with new powers of invention. "Somebody's stopping by to see me tonight. He'll be arriving at any minute."

Damion's arms fell to his sides. "Somebody's coming to see you, and you forgot to mention it until now? Who is it, for God's sake?"

That was a very good question. Who on earth could she claim was coming to visit her when it was already approaching midnight?

"It's Adam," she gasped. "Adam Hunter. You remember him." The lie sprang to her lips with disconcerting ease. "He has some important papers he wants me to sign, and I asked him to stop by after the party."

At that precise moment the intercom buzzed, and she almost fell over her own feet in her eagerness to answer it. She hoped it wasn't somebody ringing her bell by mistake. She needed an excuse to invite somebody—almost anybody—up to her apartment. She was panting as she leaned against the wall and pressed the speaker button.

"Hello," she said eagerly.

"Lynn? It's Adam. Are you alone?"

"Adam!" She was too relieved to feel surprised at the sound of his voice, too relieved even to feel shock because her lie had so unexpectedly come true. "I'm not alone," she said. "Damion's with me."

"I have to come up and see you," he said. "I've been trying to reach you all evening, but you didn't answer your phone, and then it was taken off the hook. I have something important to discuss with you, Lynn."

At that moment she wouldn't have cared if all he wanted to discuss was the requirements of the New York transportation system for the year 2000.

"Come on up," she said. "Damion was just about to leave anyway."

She released the button, cutting off the connection, then turned slowly around. Damion was standing in the center of the room, looking at her. For once his eyes didn't appear dazzling; they merely looked shrewd.

"That was Adam Hunter," she said, twisting her hands nervously in front of her. "You remember I mentioned he would be stopping by tonight."

Damion began to rebutton his shirt. "Yes," he said. "I realized you were speaking with Adam Hunter."

She walked over to the table, found his cuff links, and handed them to him in silence.

"Thank you," he said, dropping them into his pocket.

"Damion, I'm sorry. Things kind of got out of hand between us."

"I'm not sure what you're apologizing for."

They were interrupted by the chime of the doorbell. When she opened the apartment door, Adam entered, halting abruptly when he saw Damion pulling on his discarded evening jacket.

Adam's eyes glittered with opaque brilliance, and

he nodded curtly in Damion's direction. "Hello, Mr. Tanner. Are you leaving?" The words, though polite, weren't really a question.

"Yes, I'm leaving."

"I'm sure you won't mind if I say a proper hello to my fiancée, will you? I've been waiting all day to be with her."

Adam must have felt Lynn's startled jump, for he squeezed her hand warningly. Then, without giving her or Damion a chance to say anything, he swung her around in his arms and put his hand under her chin, tilting her face gently upward.

"Hello, darling," he murmured.

She gulped. "H-hello."

"I've missed you, Lynn." He sighed with the heart-rending gruffness of a man scarcely able to control his feelings. "By lunchtime I was already wondering how I would make it through to the end of the day."

Too busy commanding her knees to stop shaking, she couldn't speak. She reminded herself that he was only acting, but the reminder didn't seem to have much effect on her accelerating pulse. Involuntarily she closed her eyes as she felt his hand caress her cheek, his sensitive fingers stroking along the soft curve of her jaw and down to her throat. Her head fell back against his arm, and she felt the whisper of his breath touch her face. Her heart began to thump in unison with her quivering knees as she waited for his kiss.

His mouth was warm and achingly tender as he parted her lips. Just for an instant it seemed that he was kissing her with a deep, yearning hunger, and her body responded, melting against him in undeniable surrender. But he ended the embrace as swiftly as it had begun. He lifted his head and rested his forehead briefly against hers, then he patted her shoulder and walked briskly toward the shelf where she kept her supply of drinks and glasses. His back toward the center of the room, he poured himself some club soda.

Lynn's breathing gradually returned to normal. The whole episode had lasted only a few moments. To Damion their kiss had probably seemed too brief to be anything more than a casual greeting. To Adam the kiss had presumably been nothing more than a move in the game they had both agreed he should play. But for her, it had been a devastating revelation of the true state of her feelings.

Lynn brushed a curl away from her face with an impatient, half-angry gesture. She realized belatedly that Damion and Adam had already exchanged courteous good nights and that Damion was now approaching her.

She smiled at him with all the brightness she could muster. "Sorry we had to cut short our evening, Damion, but I'm sure you understand how it is." She gestured vaguely toward Adam. "You know, the papers I have to sign and everything."

"Yes, I think I do understand." Damion slung his white silk evening scarf around his neck and dropped his overcoat over his arm. "Good night, Lynn," he said, taking her hand between both of his. "I'll see you in the office tomorrow morning."

"Yes, I'll be there at eight. I still have some correspondence to catch up on. Thank you for a very enjoyable evening, Damion."

"It was definitely my pleasure. Like I told you before, you're a terrific dancer and a great companion. It certainly made a pleasant change to go out with a woman who wasn't constantly worrying if her best facial angle was turned toward the cameras."

"Maybe you should try it more often," she suggested softly.

"Maybe I should. Good night, Lynn."

CHAPTER SEVEN

SHE CLOSED THE front door behind him and slumped against it in momentary relief before walking back into the living room. Adam was seated on the sofa, sipping his drink. His face was in profile, and the overhead lamp left his features in shadow. From what she could see, however, he didn't look like a man who had just made any earth-shaking discoveries about the woman he'd kissed. If anything, he looked faintly preoccupied, as if he were mentally reviewing a complex financial statement for one of his projects.

The air of preoccupation was replaced with a friendly smile when she sat down in the armchair near the sofa.

"I'm sorry to turn up on your doorstep at such an unreasonable hour," he said. "I hope I didn't ruin anything for you and Damion."

"No, no, it's no problem." She pleated a fold of beige lace between her fingers, then smoothed it out again. "Although I don't understand why you told Damion we were engaged. It's one thing to pique his interest with a little jealousy, but to claim we're getting married was ridiculous, Adam. Apart from anything else, he's not the sort of man who would start an affair with another man's fiancée. Another man's girl friend, yes, but not somebody who was already committed to marriage."

"I'm sorry, Lynn. The fact is, I spoke and acted without thinking just now. I guess you could say that I got carried away in the heat of the moment. I've never understood what that expression means before, but I do now."

She heard the thread of self-derision in his words, even though she couldn't understand its cause. "You sound like a virtuous Victorian maiden protesting on the morning after," she said, trying to match his mood.

The taut lines of his mouth relaxed into a fleeting smile. "You know, these past few days I've begun to wonder whether I might have missed my true vocation. Do you think the stage lost a second Laurence Olivier when I decided to become an accountant? I've really enjoyed playing the part of your lover. Have you noticed how good I'm getting at smoldering?"

She glanced up, startled by his question, and found his gaze fixed on her mouth, his eyes burning with the white heat of naked physical desire. For a heart-stopping moment, their gazes remained locked, then he closed his eyes briefly. When he opened them again she saw nothing in his expression but a hint of friendly laughter.

"Aren't you impressed?" he asked lightly. "I bet you never suspected I had that much acting talent."

She swallowed hard. "No, I didn't. I'm very impressed," she said in a small voice. "And I'm grateful for all the time you've spent with me over the past few days. I'm glad you haven't found your role too tedious."

"Not at all." He stared down at the ice cubes melting in his glass. "In fact, I've thrown myself into the role with such a vengeance that I actually felt jealous when I found Damion up here with you, making himself at home. For at least two seconds I was contemplating murder."

He broke into laughter, tacitly inviting her to share the joke, but she couldn't manage to produce more than a weak smile. She thought of a dozen different responses and discarded them all, remaining awkwardly silent. For a woman who five days ago had considered Adam the easiest person in the world to talk to, the sudden number of taboo subjects between them was extraordinary.

"What did you want to speak to me about?" she asked finally. "It must have been important to bring you over here at this hour."

His hesitation was so slight that she scarcely noticed it. "Yes, it was. I had a phone call from your father earlier this evening."

She felt her cheeks pale. "Nothing's wrong at home, is it?"

"No, nothing at all," he reassured her. "Your parents are both fine. In fact, in some ways, you could say your father had good news to report. He's had an offer to buy Wisteria Inn, for almost fifteen thousand dollars more than I'd estimated he could reasonably expect."

For a minute she was too stunned to speak. "Dad and Mom are selling the inn?" she said when she finally recovered her breath.

"They've been thinking about selling it for quite a while now."

She was conscious of a sensation of wrenching loss, followed by hurt. "They told you, but they didn't tell me? Adam, for heaven's sake, I've spent at least one weekend a month with them during the past year. Why didn't they ever mention anything about their plans to sell?"

He was silent for a moment. "There were several reasons," he said, "but chiefly they didn't say anything because they didn't want to worry you."

"Worry me?" Her feeling that Adam wasn't telling the whole truth returned in full force. "Adam, please answer me honestly. My mother and father are both okay, aren't they? I mean, neither of them has some illness they don't want me to know about?"

"I promise you, Lynn, that they're both every bit as healthy as they look. I imagine your mother will still be baking the world's best blueberry crumble when she's ninety, and your dad will still be claiming he's caught New England's largest trout. But they've been running the inn together for over thirty-five years, and quite simply, they'd like to retire and take things a bit easier. Your dad wants to go fishing with my dad whenever the fancy takes him, and your mother wants to spend some time sitting in a comfortable armchair, improving her needlepoint designs. You know she's had her eye on that national competition for the last couple of years, and next year she's determined to win it. They've been successful entrepreneurs for a long time, and they've decided they'd like to sit back and enjoy the rewards of their years of hard work."

"But, Adam, they love Wisteria Inn! It was in Dad's family for three generations before he and my mother converted it into a hotel. I can't imagine them living contentedly anywhere else."

"Yes," he said quietly, "they do love living there. That's one of the reasons it's taken them such a long time to decide that they really must sell. They're not sick, Lynn, but they're not young people anymore. Running an inn is demanding work, physically and mentally."

"But I don't understand why they didn't tell me. Why do you know so much about them that I don't? You're an old family friend, Adam, but I'm their only daughter!"

"They didn't expect matters to come to a head quite so swiftly."

There was a touch of defiance in the tilt of her chin when she looked at him. "I want you to answer me honestly, Adam. Why do I get the feeling recently that I've been moving through my life in a pleasant, brightly-colored haze, while all around me people in the real world have been organizing themselves so as to avoid bursting my bubble and revealing to me the unpleasant fact that the world is often drab and colorless? Do I give the impression of being so fragile or so unfeeling that my own parents can't even confide in me when they want to retire?"

"You're not unfeeling at all, quite the contrary. You have a melting heart and a tendency to try to help the whole world solve its hurts. From your parents' point of view, that's the major part of their problem."

He got up and walked over to her fish tank, staring at the bright neons and elegant angelfish as they darted in and out among the plastic water weeds. "Lynn, I don't have to remind you that your parents are very special people. They're extremely sensitive to the fact that you're an only child, born late in their lives. The last thing they want is to burden you with choices and decisions that you make for their sake and not for yourself. Of course they would prefer to continue living at the inn, if the responsibility for day-to-day management could be taken from their shoulders. Of course they would prefer not to sell a house that's been home to your father's family for nearly a hundred and fifty years. But they refused point-blank to allow me to discuss the sale with you, because they were afraid you'd volunteer to take over the running of the inn. The fact is, they were sure you'd make the offer only for their sake, not for your own, and they don't want you to make that sacrifice."

"They were so certain that they didn't even feel the need to ask me?"

"They believe that you love living in Manhattan and that your career in the entertainment industry is very important to you. They don't want to present you with an impossible choice between your sense of duty and what they think you really want to do."

Her head jerked up. "Is that why you were asking me all those questions about my future career plans the other night?"

"Partly. I knew this offer was in the works, and I wondered if there was any point in mentioning it to you. At the time I decided there wasn't." He smiled slightly. "It seemed clear to me that your heart was still deeply buried in greasepaint."

A touch of bitterness tinged her answering smile. "And God forbid that I should be presented with any difficult choices. I mean, what does my parents' happiness count for in comparison to my desire to continue working in the entertainment industry? What's forty years of my parents' lives in comparison to my need to work in a glamorous industry."

He regarded her, considering. "I think you're underselling yourself, Lynn. I did try to persuade your parents to tell you what was going on. It was because they were so sure you'd volunteer to take over the inn that they refused to let you in on their plans."

"To be honest, I don't know who I'm most angry with, me or you. Or maybe even my parents. I'm furious with myself for being so unobservant. I'm angry with Mom and Dad for not recognizing that I have a stake in this decision, not to mention the fact that I care about their future happiness. And I'm angry with you because you didn't take matters into your own hands and explain what was going on."

"It was impossible for me to betray your parents' confidence, Lynn. They consulted me in my professional capacity, not only as a friend."

She sighed. "You're right. I guess I'm yelling at you because I'm mad at myself. But I still don't see the reason for this sudden frantic rush to inform me about what's going on. For months nobody has bothered to tell me anything at all. Why at midnight on this particular Thursday does the situation suddenly become so urgent that you have to come dashing around to my apartment just to tell me about it?"

He seemed preoccupied with dropping a pinch of fish food into the tank. He was silent as he watched two of the angelfish gobble it down. Lynn had already sensed something unusual in his manner, and this time his hesitation was too pronounced to ignore. She had a strong feeling that, rather than telling her the real reason for his visit, he was merely searching for an explanation that would be logical enough to satisfy her. And yet she was sure he wouldn't lie about her parents' health, and she couldn't think of anything else he might want to conceal.

"Adam," she repeated, "why did you have to come here at midnight to tell me all this?"

"The prospective buyers made their offer at noon today, and they placed a time limit on the offer," he said abruptly. "It expires at five o'clock on Saturday afternoon. When your father called me this evening, I convinced him that it was unfair to make such an important decision without consulting you. Despite what you indicated to me the other night about your long-term career plans, I think you're entitled to be given a clear-cut choice: Your parents will refuse this offer for the inn if you're prepared to come home and manage it on their behalf. They would pay you two thousand dollars a year more than you're currently earning, and we would work out together some scheme for gradually turning over the equity to you, while ensuring that they retain a comfortable retirement income. I thought you would need some time to think about the offer, which is why I interrupted your date with Damion Tanner. There aren't many hours until the Comptex offer expires. Are you interested in the idea of taking over the management of the hotel, Lynn?"

She was seized by a surge of longing so strong that she almost forgot the suspicion that Adam was not being completely honest with her. Nostalgic mental pictures of Wisteria Inn were quickly tempered by a sharp flare of excitement. Running the inn, she realized, would utilize many of the administrative and organizational skills that were underemployed in her current job. At the same time it would provide new scope for her creative talents. Having grown up watching her parents' management style, she knew there was a definite element of showmanship in the running of a successful family inn. She had never really had a chance to explore the limits of her own creative abilities. Working for Damion required constant subjugation of her personality to his creative needs, while running the inn would give almost limitless scope to her own unique talents.

Taking over the inn would also solve the dilemma of what to do about her job with Damion. With a flash of stark self-knowledge she realized that, even if the sale of the inn hadn't come up, she still wouldn't have wanted to move with him to Hollywood. She assessed her feelings with a ruthless honesty that was entirely new and realized that she no longer had any desire for a personal relationship with Damion Tanner. Much as she admired his talents as an actor, she was un-impressed with his skills as a human being.

The thoughts rushed helter-skelter through her mind while Adam waited patiently for her response. She had no idea what to say to him. The previous weekend she had breathlessly confided that she was madly in love with Damion. What would he think if she now admitted that she wasn't in love with Damion at all? What *could* he think, other than that she was an im-mature, irresponsible, imperceptive person? Could she agree to take over the inn without revealing that Damion was no longer a factor in her plans?

"You're taking a long time to give me an answer," Adam said softly.

"It's not easy to know what to say." She stared down at her hands, hoping for an inspiration that didn't come. Quite apart from the complexities of her re-lationship with Adam, it was tough to make such an important career decision with so little time for re-flection. The inn represented a thirty-year investment of her parents' talents and a lifelong investment of their savings, and she wasn't sure that she had the management skills to operate it profitably. It would be dreadful if she took over the management, then ran their investment into the ground.

"I need more information, Adam," she said, play-ing for time. "This isn't an easy decision to reach. When do my parents need an answer?"

"As I told you, the official deadline on the offer is Saturday afternoon. I'm meeting early tomorrow evening with some of the senior officials of Comptex, the corporation making the bid. Their headquarters are located in New Jersey, near Princeton, where they've built their flagship hotel. Would you like to come with me? Meeting some of the Comptex executives might give you a better feel for the changes they would make at Wisteria Inn, and that might help you to reach a decision."

"Yes," she said, sighing with relief. At least she would have a few hours to get her chaotic feelings into some sort of order. "That sounds like a great idea, Adam. What time should I be ready?"

"I ought to pick you up by three-thirty if we're going to get out of the city before the rush hour traffic becomes impossible. Can you get away from the office by then?"

"Yes. I'll explain to Damion how important it is for me to leave early. He'll understand."

"It's all settled then." He glanced at his watch. "It's nearly one o'clock. You'd better get some sleep, or you won't be needing any more of that purple eyeliner to give you interesting shadows around your eyes."

"Is that a polite way of telling me I look haggard?"

His gaze ran over her briefly, and for an instant she glimpsed some dark emotion behind the blankness of his eyes, then it was gone.

"You don't look haggard," he said, his voice flat. He picked up his jacket and walked to the door. Automatically she followed him. His hand slipped around her shoulders, pulling her toward him in a careless gesture he had used a thousand times before. But tonight her head went back as he leaned over her, and she closed her eyes, feeling her body tremble as she waited for his kiss.

His lips brushed casually against her cheek. They were very cool and very impersonal.

"Good night, Lynn. Sleep well." His voice radiated friendliness. "I'll look forward to seeing you tomorrow."

He was out of her apartment before she could drag open her eyes. She closed the door, but she didn't slip the bolt into place until the sound of his footsteps had completely died away. She latched the chain onto the hook, then put her hand to her lips. They felt swollen and hot, even though Adam hadn't touched them. She felt her cheeks. They were on fire. Two nights ago she had managed to convince herself that she didn't want Adam to kiss her. Tonight she abandoned even the pretense of pretending.

Minutes ticked by, endless and uncounted, before she finally found the willpower to move. She walked back to the sofa and pulled it out into the sleeping position. She brushed her teeth and washed her face, then returned to the bed and stood looking at the pillows, not really seeing them.

She flopped onto the mattress and stared at the ceiling. She probably had the only apartment in Manhattan without any cracks in the ceiling. She was probably the only woman in Manhattan who imagined herself in love with one man on Saturday and with a different man on the following Thursday. Particularly when the second man had been her best friend since before she started high school.

She rolled over onto her stomach, wondering if anybody had ever actually died of frustrated physical desire. She would have to remember to look it up in the almanac or the encyclopedia or somewhere. She suspected she was about to become the first entry in a whole new set of statistics. Because if Adam didn't kiss her—really kiss her—tomorrow night, there was a distinct possibility that her body would explode.

She listened to her heart as it pounded against the blankets and wondered how long a heart could beat at double its normal rate before dire consequences set in. She hoped very much that her heart could hold out for another twenty-four hours. She needed to survive at least that long if Adam was to make love to her.

The alarm went off at six in the morning, but she didn't need it. It had seemed a very long night.

CHAPTER EIGHT

BY THE TIME she reached the office, Lynn had brought her feelings for Damion into startlingly clear perspective. The simple truth was that she had been blinded all these months by her admiration for his acting ability. He *was* a wonderful actor, probably one of the very best working in television today, and one of the few equally at home on the screen and on the stage.

She had fallen in love with Damion the actor, and it had taken her ten months to realize that Damion the man didn't interest her in the slightest. All his energies were channeled into his roles, leaving almost nothing for the person outside the actor. His emotions were rarely more than hand-me-downs from the parts he played. When he spoke, subconsciously he was addressing an audience. When he moved, subconsciously he was assessing camera angles. The only

time he became wholly himself was when he discussed
the technical aspects of his profession. When he had
told her about his refusal to escort Tiffany Brandon
to the movie premiere, it was the first time that she
had ever seen Damion the man step back and assess
the sacrifices he was making in order to be Damion
the actor.

His professional dedication had probably kept the
scales on her eyes for so long, Lynn thought. Damion
respected her judgment and relied on her professional
opinions. In a way he had revealed more of his true
character to her than he did to most people. When she
considered her own frustrated ambitions as an actress
and combined them with Damion's outstanding talent
and stunning good looks, it was perhaps no wonder
that she had failed to see the wood for the lushness
of the trees. She was embarrassed, however, to think
that she had imagined herself in love on such totally
inadequate grounds.

Betty arrived promptly at eight. "You look hollow-
cheeked, pale, and miserable," she said. "Lord, am
I envious! How did you do it? Only a week ago you
looked disgustingly healthy and quite cheerful."

Lynn's laugh contained a faint trace of hysteria. "I
fell in love," she said, admitting the truth to Betty
even as she admitted it to herself. "I'm twenty-six
years old, and I just realized I've been in love with
the same man for years. Isn't it ironic?"

"It depends on whether or not he loves you in
return."

"Of course he doesn't, or at least not in the right
way. He considers me his best friend. When we're
together we reminisce about things—the time he
helped me bury my pet toad, or the time I fell into
the local mud puddle." She gave another painful gasp

of laughter. "Betty, I think I'm going to disintegrate into small pieces if he gives me one more friendly thump on the shoulders."

Betty examined her contemplatively, then grinned. "I'd be more sympathetic if unrequited love wasn't making you look so gorgeous. Lynn, honey, if the man hasn't noticed that you're just about vibrating with suppressed sexual tension, then he must be blind. If I were you, next time he starts talking about toads, I'd switch the conversation to their mating habits. I understand some of them stay clasped flipper to flipper for several days."

"Toads don't have flippers."

"Your problem, Lynn, is that you get hung up on trivia."

The buzzer on Lynn's intercom called her into Damion's office. When she entered his room, he was standing next to one of the windows, looking more handsome than usual as the early morning sunlight glanced off his ebony hair.

She placed a stack of fan mail on his desk, along with her replies. "This is all from people in various hospitals," she said. "I've prepared the standard letter, but I think you might want to sign some of them personally."

"Yes, I'll get to it later on this morning. Lynn, would you like to have dinner with me tonight? Somewhere quiet, just the two of us?"

She drew in a deep breath. "Thank you very much for the invitation, Damion, but I really do have to go out tonight. It's a business dinner connected with the possible sale of my parents' inn."

"How about tomorrow night?"

"I guess not, Damion. Thank you again, but I'm spending the weekend with my parents."

"And with your old friend Adam Hunter."

She felt her cheeks flame with color. "Yes, with Adam, too."

Damion stepped across to his desk, read the topmost letter, and scrawled his signature at the foot of the page. Then he glanced up and smiled a touch ruefully. "I had an interesting ride home from your apartment last night," he said. "I calculated that there are about three million single women living in the New York City area, and that probably a quarter of a million of them are passably good-looking. I estimated that at least a hundred thousand are stunning to look at, and that maybe twenty thousand are stunning to look at *and* reasonably intelligent. I decided that I'm not going to waste my time worrying about the one woman out of three million who got away. And you did get away, didn't you, Lynn?"

"Yes," she said softly. "But I've enjoyed working with you, Damion."

"Past tense?"

"I don't think I want to move to Hollywood, and you need somebody who's prepared to commute. Betty can hold down the fort here most of the time, but you need an assistant who's happy to be in New York City one week and L.A. the next. I'm genuinely flattered by your offer to take charge of setting up your West Coast office, but I have things I want to do here—a couple of new directions in my career that I'd like to think about pursuing. Of course I'll stay on as long as it takes to find my replacement, and I'll help train her, if you'd like that."

"Yes, I'd like that." His smile was tinged with wry self-awareness. "Julie Blake is going to be my next leading lady," he said, naming one of Hollywood's hottest superstars, known internationally for her explosive combination of intense emotional profundity and steaming, sensual good looks. "It promises to be an interesting few months' filming, don't you think?"

"Very interesting," she replied, smiling.

She worked for the rest of the day at an even more intense pace than usual, anxious to finish up as many tasks as possible before leaving for the Comptex meeting with Adam. At three-fifteen she tore into the bathroom and freshened up, and at three-thirty she arrived in the downstairs lobby. Adam was already parked outside the entrance, leaning against the gleaming door of his silver Firebird. He looked tanned, spare, and devastatingly sexy. As Lynn walked across the carpeted lobby, she suddenly realized why he had looked so different to her recently. After years of viewing him with the eyes of a young girl, she was finally allowing herself to see him with the eyes of a woman. And what she saw nearly took her breath away.

He was not looking in her direction and didn't notice her arrival.

"I made it on time," she said, touching him lightly on the arm. "I've left chaos behind me, but here I am!"

He swung around, his eyes raking her, and she felt prickles of desire tingle all over her skin.

"I'm glad you could get away," he said evenly. "The traffic's bad already."

Simple words, casually spoken, but her new self-awareness seemed to have given her a whole new perspective on the world. She would have staked her life on the fact that it cost Adam some effort to sound so calm.

They said little during the long drive. His attention appeared fully focused on weaving the car in and out of the snarled lines of traffic. She wiled away the time concocting plans for the evening, once the meeting with Comptex was over.

She was relieved once the exhaust fumes and blaring horns of the tunnel and turnpike were behind them, and they could escape onto the slightly less crowded highway leading to Princeton. Comptex Corporation's headquarters was located in a pleasant suburban setting, next to their flagship hotel. Both building complexes were surrounded by lavishly landscaped grounds. Formal fountains decorated the lawn in front of the corporate headquarters, and a nine-hole golf course stretched out to the rear of the hotel. Late-blooming chrysanthemums, laid out in neat rows, decorated the driveway leading to both complexes.

The Senior Vice President in charge of Corporate Development, the Vice President of Corporate Finance, and the Vice President of Legal Affairs met Lynn and Adam in the lobby and conducted them into one of the corporate meeting rooms, a cavernous square space decorated with a great deal of fake oak paneling and large crystal chandeliers. After the necessary introductions had been made, they seated themselves around a circular table and smiled at each other over pristine white notepads and glasses of ice water.

All three executives were competent, affable, smiling gentlemen who made no secret of the fact that Comptex was excited at the prospect of buying Wisteria Inn. They had decided, the Senior Vice President informed Lynn, to develop a chain of personally-managed "individualized" inns. The personal touch, he said earnestly, was going to be the hallmark of the hotel industry in the future, and Comptex planned to be at the cutting edge of hotel industry changes.

"It's an interesting idea," Adam remarked. "You mean that individual local managers will have almost complete control over how the inns are run?"

"Oh, no!" The Vice President of Corporate Finance sounded horrified at the suggestion. "You see, that's the whole beauty of the chain concept, Mr. Hunter. Management retains central control of finances, inventory, purchasing, and so on, thus ensuring optimum efficiency of our systems. Comptex guests will be able to go from one inn to the next always knowing exactly what they'll find. Hotel guests don't like surprises."

"I understand that part of the concept," Lynn said. "But where does the personal management come in? My parents have worked for a long time to develop a very special country atmosphere at Wisteria Inn. How are you planning to preserve that special character and style?"

The Vice President of Legal Affairs linked his hands over his ample stomach. "We're selecting our acquisitions very carefully to ensure a certain inevitable integrity of individual architectural style," he said, his smile only a touch patronizing when he regarded Lynn. "Our current corporate planning envisages maximum enhancement of the unique external visual impact on arriving guests."

"In plain English does that mean you want all the inn exteriors to look different?"

The Senior Vice President beamed. "Exactly, Miss Frampton. And in addition to the unique external appearance our on-the-spot managers will be able to decide on all those important little local touches, like the color of the flowers for the entrance lobby and the local House Specialty on the dinner menu. We're all very excited about our concept, Miss Frampton. Individualization and standardization working in harmony at last."

"It certainly sounds like a fascinating slogan," she murmured.

After a further half-hour of similar questions and non-answers, the Vice President of Finance conducted them on a tour of the neighboring hotel where, he said, the new individualization process was already in successful operation.

To Comptex, individualization apparently meant that each bedroom should be painted a slightly different color and that the bedspreads in each room should be dyed to match the walls. On the higher floors the rooms were larger, and in each of them, an arrangement of silk flowers, placed meticulously dead center on the imitation-walnut table, echoed the predominant color scheme. The flowers, the Vice President explained proudly, had been the idea of their in-house decorator. The white-tiled bathrooms, he apologized, had not yet been changed to incorporate the new, personalized look.

Lynn eventually felt compelled to point out that patrons only slept in one bedroom at a time, and so they would never know what color the other rooms were painted. The elaborate variations in paint shade, which had absolutely zero effect on the basic amenities of the room, therefore seemed rather pointless. The Vice President of Finance regarded her with a mixture of agitation and blank incomprehension. Adam grinned and shrugged. She decided not to pursue her point.

Their tour was completed in the main floor bar, where localization meant having one wall covered by a large photographic mural of Princeton University and personalization meant having the waiters introduce themselves by name. The Senior Vice President urged them most cordially to spend the night in the hotel as guests of Comptex Corporation. Lynn expelled a huge sigh of relief when Adam politely but firmly declined the offer.

They made no comment on the pomposity of their hosts until they had completed the ritual exchange of polite good-byes and were seated in the car, speeding back toward Manhattan.

"Your father won't get a better price from anybody else," Adam said eventually. "In fact, he probably won't get nearly as much. Comptex is prepared to pay generously for 'individual architectural integrity.'"

"But it's unbearable to think of those people running Wisteria Inn. It's like inviting vandals to come in and devastate your home."

"I've met people who've dealt with Comptex Corporation before," Adam said. "I had a good idea of the sort of plans they would have lined up for the inn. I may as well admit that my motives in taking you with me tonight weren't entirely pure. I guessed what your reaction to their various vice presidents was likely to be, and I counted on that to help sway your decision."

In the dark car it was impossible to discern his expression. "You sound as if you have a personal involvement in what I decide to do, Adam," she said softly.

He switched lanes before answering her. "Wisteria Inn has been like a second home to me, and your parents are dear friends," he said composedly. "Of course I care what happens to their inn."

"That was a non-answer to my question worthy of a Comptex executive."

"All right," he said shortly. "I think you should consider long and hard before you allow Wisteria Inn to pass out of your family. At this moment you may feel reluctant to give up your...association...with Damion Tanner. But later on I think you might bitterly regret losing the inn."

It wasn't the answer she had wanted him to give, since it revealed absolutely nothing of his personal feelings toward her. How crazy it was, she thought, that she was sitting in a car next to the person she had once imagined she knew best in the world, and she hadn't the faintest idea what he really felt about her.

"Time is beginning to run out on the Comptex contract," Adam said. "I don't want to pressure you, Lynn, but do you feel able to make a decision on the offer your parents made? Do you have any interest in taking over the management of the inn?"

She had to bite her tongue to stop herself from saying yes, of course she was interested, that of course she would take the job. The trouble was, she knew there was no way she could express her enthusiasm without causing Adam to ask several awkward questions about her plans for the future and several even more awkward questions about the state of her relationship with Damion. She wasn't yet ready to reveal how shallow and immature her feelings for Damion had actually been. During the past week she had discovered that Adam's respect was vitally important to her, and she didn't see how he could possibly respect a woman who claimed to be desperately in love on Saturday, and six days later was announcing it had all been an unfortunate mistake.

There was another good reason for her hesitation. If she seemed uncertain of her decision about the inn, she would have a perfect excuse for inviting Adam up to her apartment once they arrived back in the city. She could claim that she needed his advice to make up her mind.

It was ironic to think that she had to invent reasons

for inviting Adam up to her apartment, but during the long wakeful hours of the previous night, she had discovered several interesting truths about their relationship.

One of those truths was that in recent years they had almost never spent time alone with each other. True, Adam often called for her at her apartment, but he rarely came inside, and even when he did, until this past week he had never stayed more than a few minutes. They spent weekends at her parents' inn, and they went fishing together or took drives through the local countryside. But they had only rarely shared a dinner date, and they had never spent an evening without other people within close calling distance.

She had never been inside Adam's apartment on Park Avenue, although he had lived in the same building for nearly five years. She realized now that the omission had been deliberate on his part. Several times she had suggested cooking a meal for him either at her apartment or at his. She had occasionally suggested renting a movie and running it through his video machine. He'd always turned aside her suggestions with a counter-suggestion that they visit a new restaurant or take in a movie playing somewhere on the other side of town. His refusals had been couched in such skillful terms that she was only now beginning to realize how cleverly he had curtailed their intimacy.

"Hey, Lynn, have you fallen asleep? Did you hear me ask you a question about managing Wisteria Inn?"

Adam's voice sounded warm, friendly, and familiar, but the feelings it aroused in her were totally new and almost frightening in their intensity.

"I'm not asleep," she said, hoping her voice didn't sound as strained to him as it did to her. "I was trying to think logically, which probably accounts for my pained expression."

"And did you succeed? Have you reached any decisions?"

She sighed. "Not really. It's awfully difficult to know what I ought to do, especially since I'm trying to think on an empty stomach. I worked through lunch at the office today, and we haven't had anything to eat tonight except some peanuts when that miserable vice president took us for a drink. Would you like to come back to my apartment? I have ham and eggs and a bottle of Chenin Blanc. I could whip us both up an omelet."

His answer was so smooth that five days earlier she wouldn't have noticed the fractional hesitation before he replied. "Thanks, but I won't take you up on the offer, Lynn. It'll be ten o'clock before we're back at your apartment. That's too late for you to start cooking a meal."

"I'll be cooking for myself in any case, so an extra person won't make the slightest difference. Please, Adam, it's Friday night. Who wants to eat dinner alone? And, besides, I badly need your advice. As you pointed out yourself, time's running out on us as far as Comptex is concerned."

The silence in the car was suddenly charged with tension, then he gave her an easy smile, making her wonder if once again she had projected her own feelings onto Adam. "You know me," he said. "I'm an easy prey for anybody asking for advice. I'm always delighted to listen to myself being profound. But it would be better if we ate out, Lynn. That way we can concentrate on our discussion without worrying about what's burning in the kitchen. There's a great little French restaurant around the corner from my apartment. Why don't we eat there?"

Because there are no beds in the darn French restaurant, she thought with frustration. Because I want to see you when your eyes are blind with passion, not opaque with hidden emotions or silver with silent laughter.

She forced her mouth into a sweet, slightly hurt smile. "For some reason I don't feel in the mood for eating out tonight. Besides, my cooking's so much better these days, I'd enjoy preparing a meal for us. You ought to let me show you how much I've improved. Mom's been teaching me determinedly for the past year. I think she was beginning to feel that my lack of skill in the kitchen was hindering me in my quest for a husband." She gave him another artless smile, one she felt sure her drama coach would have been proud of. "Please, Adam, I'd like to surprise you with how good I am. As a cook, I mean."

His hands tightened on the wheel, and his reply came out just a shade faster than normal. "All right, if you insist. We'll eat at your apartment, if that's what you want."

He circled the block twice looking for a parking space, but in the end he had to leave his car in a garage more than three blocks from her building. The moon was covered in heavy black clouds when they left the car, and the wind buffeted them as they walked up the exit ramp. She shivered as they hurried along the sidewalk. The temperature had dropped precipitously since they'd left town earlier that afternoon.

They were still two blocks from her apartment when lightning arched across the sky, followed almost immediately by a deafening clap of thunder. Within seconds the heavens opened, sluicing the streets with sheets of blowing, bitterly cold rain.

Adam put his arm around Lynn's waist, and they ran through the downpour. The wind forced the rain directly into their faces, making it difficult to see. Struggling to keep up with Adam, she stepped carelessly, plunging her foot into a puddle of muddy water that had collected in a shallow pothole. She wrenched her ankle, snapping the heel of her shoe as she pulled it free and losing her balance.

Only Adam's tight grip around her waist prevented her from falling. He half-carried her toward the awning of a building, and she leaned against the wall, pushing her dripping wet hair out of her eyes. He stood in front of her, his hands braced against the wall, shielding her from the worst of the rain. No part of his body touched hers, but his breath warmed her cheek, and she could feel heat steal down from her face and begin to pound through her veins.

"Are you all right?" he asked. His voice held concern, but she could detect no other emotion. "Will you be able to walk?"

She closed her eyes, afraid of what they might reveal to him. She had made so many misjudgments recently. What if she was wrong in thinking Adam was physically attracted to her? What if he felt absolutely nothing for her but the affection of long-standing friendship? At this precise moment it certainly didn't look as if he felt anything but the normal concern of an old and dear friend. He didn't look like a man whose pulses were throbbing and whose heart was pounding with frustrated passion. Maybe he didn't go for the drowned rat look, she thought, biting back a sob that contained both tears and laughter.

"I'm fine," she said, pushing a sopping strand of hair out of her eyes. "But I think I'll have to hop all the way home."

"I could try to break off the other heel."

"I don't think that would work. They never break when you want them to." She forced a teasing note into her voice, although the effort nearly choked her.

"I can walk if you'll lend me your strong shoulder to lean on."

They were soaked by the time they reached her apartment building. He pushed her ahead of him into the lobby and summoned the elevator. While they waited for it to arrive, she tried to concentrate on picking a few dead leaves from her jacket. She was panting slightly, she supposed from the effort of running two blocks in broken shoes. Water dripped off her wet skirt in a cold stream, forming a muddy puddle at her feet. Another puddle formed to the right of her. She glanced up, registering the fact that Adam was every bit as wet as she was.

The elevator arrived, and they stepped into it. Silence enveloped them both with a deadening, suffocating weight. Adam crossed to her side, but his expression was inscrutable as he picked a dead leaf from her hair.

"You have a smudge of dirt on your nose," he said.

"That's Manhattan for you." She tried to smile. "Even the rainwater is full of soot."

The elevator reached the seventh floor, and she pulled out her key, hurrying ahead of him along the short corridor. He closed the apartment door behind them, and she flipped on the overhead light. His blond hair was plastered to his head, making his features appear more austere than usual, and his mouth was touched by deep lines of weariness or perhaps tension. It required intense physical control on her part not to reach up and run her fingers over those hard lines.

She walked quickly out of the tiny entrance, away from temptation. "I'm going to take a hot shower," she said. "I'm absolutely drenched. You can take one as soon as I'm through, Adam. I'll only be two minutes."

"Take your time. I'll open the wine while I'm waiting." He slipped off his shoes and socks. "If you can give me a towel, I'll dry my feet so I don't leave a trail of wet footprints all over your carpet."

"Sure, hang on a minute. I have a stack of clean towels in the linen closet."

She had no idea how she managed to sound so relaxed. She gave him a big beige towel, producing a wonderfully bright smile as she did so, then returned to the bathroom, stripped off her sopping clothes, and stuffed them into the laundry hamper. She stood under the shower, turning it on full force and scrubbing herself fiercely with her loofah, as if she really believed that the tingle of soap-scrubbed skin could take away the ache of sexual longing.

She toweled herself dry and combed her hair, grimacing when she glimpsed her mop of damp curls in the steamed-over bathroom mirror. During the past week her face had acquired an unexpected hint of sensuality, but her hair still looked like something straight out of a Muppets movie. She shrugged resignedly and shook talcum power over her shoulders, then slipped into her terry-cloth bathrobe, pulling the lapels close together and cinching the belt tightly around her waist.

Her body remained undeceived by the pseudo-modest gestures. Her breasts were taut against the rough terry cloth, and her skin burned with a steady inner fire. A tight belt and a high neckline offered no protection whatsoever against the clamorous demands of her senses.

"It's all yours," she said with false cheerfulness as soon as she opened the bathroom door. Her smile was so wide, she felt like an advertisement for toothpaste. She crossed the room without looking in Adam's direction and took one of her largest T-shirts from the chest of drawers.

"Take this," she said, handing it to him. "You shouldn't get back into wet clothes, but I'm afraid this is all I have that will fit you."

"It's no problem. A pair of damp trousers isn't going to kill me."

"I guess not." Her ability to smile cheerfully had finally abandoned her. She could only hope she didn't look as tense as she felt.

"The wine is open," he said. "I'll take a glass into the shower with me, if that's okay with you."

"It's fine. Dinner will be ready by the time you've finished."

As soon as the bathroom door closed behind him, she walked zombielike into the kitchen. Slumping against the counter, she leaned her forehead against one of the cabinets, grateful for its coolness against her hot skin. How could she ever have thought she was in love with Damion Tanner? she wondered. How could she have confused that mild attraction with the burning ache of the real thing? With effort she lifted her head, staring unseeingly at the calendar pinned on her wall. She wondered how she had managed to reach the ripe old age of twenty-six without ever learning that love was an emotion powerful enough to tear you apart and leave your body feeling real physical pain.

She opened the refrigerator and extracted five eggs, beating them efficiently with salt, pepper, parsley, and a little cream. At least one part of what she had told Adam tonight was true. Her cooking had improved immeasurably in the last year. She chopped four slices of ham into neat squares and put a pat of butter into the skillet but decided not to switch on the burner until Adam came out of the shower. Omelets, she had learned, couldn't be kept warm successfully.

She filled her wineglass to the brim and sipped her drink with more pleasure than usual. As soon as she finished the first glass, she poured herself a second. She had never previously understood why any sensible human being would attempt to drown his sorrows in alcohol, but at long last she was beginning to appreciate the attraction. By the end of her second glass the ache in the pit of her stomach had mellowed to a just-bearable throb of longing. Maybe three glasses would make the ache go away completely.

"Is there anything I can do to help?"

She spun around at the sound of Adam's voice, her ankle twisting clumsily beneath her. His hands reached out at once, steadying her, keeping her safe.

"Lynn, have you hurt yourself?" he asked. "Sit down for a minute so that I can check. That was quite a fall you took on the way here, and you may have sprained it."

"No, I'm sure I didn't. It isn't swollen, and it would have hurt more more before this if it was sprained."

"It'll only take a couple of seconds to check," he said. As he urged her toward one of the chairs, she gave up her attempt at resistance. His hands ran swiftly down the muscles of her calf, his fingers gentle as they pressed delicately against her instep.

"Does that hurt?" he asked.

It's agony, she wanted to say. A refined form of torture. She shifted slightly so that she could sit on her hands. That way there was no danger of finding them reaching out to run through the thick, blond strands of his hair.

"No, it doesn't hurt at all," she said. "Well, not enough to worry about anyway."

"I think it seems a bit swollen." His hands manip-

ulated her foot in a small circle, and she closed her
eyes. "Lynn?" he said. "Are you sure you're all right?"

She opened her eyes, but couldn't speak. His hand
reached up to touch her cheek, and before she realized
exactly what she was doing, she turned her head and
pressed a swift kiss against the hard curve of his palm.

"Lynn . . ." he repeated, but this time his voice
sounded harsher.

She couldn't answer him. If she spoke or even
looked at him, he would know exactly what she felt,
and she was too shy or perhaps too proud to reveal
the depth of her emotions. She knew that Adam cared
for her too much as a friend to ever hurt her willingly.
If he knew how desperately she wanted him, he might
make love to her simply to avoid wounding her feelings. And the only thing in the world worse than never
having Adam make love to her would be his making
love to her out of pity.

She heard him say her name again, and she whispered some sort of a reply, she wasn't quite sure what.
Suddenly his hands were no longer on her ankle. They
were running swiftly up her legs, stroking feverishly
over her body until they reached her face. He rose to
his feet, pulling her with him, forcing her to look at
him.

"Damn you, Lynn," he murmured. "I should never
have come here tonight."

She scarcely heard what he said. Only the urgency
of his tone penetrated the haze that enveloped her.
Desire invaded her body, making her breath hard and
uneven, her limbs soft and pliant. "Kiss me," she said.
"Please, Adam."

Her lips trembled apart as he wound his fingers
into her damp curls, holding her mouth a mere breath
away from his. For an instant his eyes blazed brilliant
silver with desire, then they closed abruptly as he

searched blindly for her mouth.

The impact of his kiss reverberated throughout her body. She tasted him on her lips, and her whole being vibrated with the intensity of her need. His tongue probed, fiercely seductive, while his lips crushed hers in endless, passionate demand. Feeling his breath shudder against her mouth, she thrust her hips hard against him, needing to feel that he wanted her, needing to know that she was desired.

He untangled his hands from her hair, sliding them urgently toward the opening of her robe. His fingers hovered over the lapels for a moment, and she waited in an agony of suspense until he pulled the robe open and curved his hands around the underside of her breasts.

He took one of her nipples into his mouth, and the pounding of the blood in her ears blocked out the sound of the rain pounding against the windows. The moist trail of his tongue left her outer skin cool but her inner flesh burning. She was shaking, and she could feel that Adam was shaking, too.

She moaned in protest when he suddenly wrenched his mouth away from hers. She reached for him, searching frantically until his hands gripped her upper arms, holding her away from his body. She heard somebody give a small whimper, and realized it was herself. Opening her eyes slowly, she struggled to bring them into focus.

Adam had turned away from her, putting the width of the small table between them. "You don't really want me to do this," he said, his voice tight with control. "You'll regret it tomorrow morning."

She blinked in bewilderment. He couldn't possibly have mistaken the passionate response of her body. How could he say she didn't want him? "I don't understand," she said. "What do you mean, Adam?"

"There are some things even your best friend can't do for you," he said flatly. "I'm sorry, Lynn, but I'm not prepared to make love to you as a stand-in for Damion Tanner. I apologize if I interrupted something important for you last night, but I won't be used to relieve a bad case of physical frustration. Maybe next week you can take up with Damion where you left off yesterday."

She felt herself pale with a mixture of white-hot anger and deep, painful hurt. "You don't have a very flattering opinion of me, do you, Adam? Do you really think I'm the sort of woman who uses lovers like interchangeable, disposable commodities? Damion didn't come up to scratch on Thursday, but what the hell, let's substitute good old Adam on Friday. Is *that* why you think I responded to your lovemaking? An acute case of overactive hormones?"

He swung around, thrusting his hands deep into the pockets of his pants, still keeping the width of the table between them. "I'm sorry, Lynn, you're right. That was insulting. I guess I'm not thinking very rationally right now."

Hurt and anger vanished in a renewed wave of longing. "Why not, Adam?" she asked quietly. "You're usually a very logical person. Why aren't you thinking rationally tonight?"

He shrugged. "It's been a tough week. My supply of rationality ran out about last Tuesday."

She looked at him, a hint of challenge in her gaze. "If I remember my Introductory Psych course correctly, people are supposed to stop thinking clearly when their emotions are involved. I'm willing to admit that I want you to make love to me, Adam. Is that what you want, too?"

His shoulders lifted in another shrug, but a brief flare of color stained his cheekbones as he moved from behind the table, allowing her a clear view of his body. "You can see that it is," he said evenly. "I want you very badly, Lynn. In fact, I want you like hell."

She closed the gap between them with a single step. Hooking her fingers into his belt buckle, she then moved her hand slowly and purposefully downward. "It certainly feels promising," she said softly.

His reaction was immediate and forceful. His breath rasped inward when she touched him, and his mouth sought hers in an explosion of renewed passion. He tore the robe from her shoulders, pushing it to the floor as he swept her into his arms. He carried her across to the sofa without ever lifting his lips from hers. She was only dimly aware of the tweed fabric of the sofa cushions scratching against her naked back, even less aware of the throw pillow he had somehow placed beneath her head. She was chiefly conscious of his lithe body, of his long, muscled length lying almost on top of her, of the feel of his hands turning her skin to rippling silk as he caressed her with skillful, supple fingers.

His mouth finally left her lips to trace an erratic path over her throat and along the hollow between her breasts. She arched in instinctive pleasure when he teased her nipples gently with his teeth, but her response quickly became too powerful for her own comfort, and she tried to push him away, frightened by the intensity of the sensations he was arousing. Her body was spiraling out of control, something that had never happened to her before.

"Oh, no, Lynn my sweet, we can't stop now," he murmured. "Things are just beginning to get interesting." His eyes laughed down at her, reassuring and arousing her at the same time. Before she could say anything, he reached out and swiftly pinned her arms over her head with one hand, while his other stroked across her hips and moved commandingly between her thighs. Laughter faded as his mouth captured hers, and he kissed her with almost bruising force.

The caress of his mouth and his hand became twin points of pleasure in a world that contained only Adam. In only a few seconds she was trembling in unison with the magic touch of his fingers, only seconds more before one wracking shudder after another convulsed her body.

Limp, sated, she floated gradually back to earth. She looked up hesitantly, embarrassed by the speed and power of her response. She found Adam gazing down at her, his eyes no longer gray and difficult to read, but hot and dark with desire. He lay propped on one elbow, his legs intimately tangled with hers on the narrow couch, his hand tracing lazy, erotic circles on her stomach. His belt buckle pressed into her waist, and the fabric of his slacks rubbed against her bare leg. Until this moment she hadn't even realized that he was still fully dressed.

She drew in a shaky breath, not quite sure if she had regained control of her vocal cords. "You should hurry up and get out of those damp clothes," she said huskily. "Didn't anybody ever tell you that you'll get rheumatism if you lie around in damp underwear?"

His mouth curved into a smile. "You'd better undress me then. I'd hate to start creaking when I move."

She slipped her hands under his borrowed T-shirt, running her mouth over his tanned skin as she pulled the shirt over his head. Once again laughter faded as quickly as it had come. When her hands fumbled with the zipper of his pants, he abandoned the pretense of waiting for her to undress him. With a quick groan of impatience, he stripped off the rest of his clothes and gathered her into his arms. He cradled her closely, flesh locked to flesh, heart beating against heart, until she felt as though her skin had fused with his, permanently and inseparably.

He placed his hands on either side of her face, holding her head still on the silk throw pillow so that she couldn't look away when he entered her. But she had no wish to disguise the shock of pleasure that ripped through her body as he thrust rhythmically inside her. She twisted under him, accommodating her softness to the driving urgency of his possession. He murmured incoherent words of love against her lips, and she drank them in, mingling his breath with her own. She wanted to tell him that she loved him, but some spark of caution held the words back; instead, she used her body to give him the message her voice was afraid to speak out loud. She wound her arms around his shoulders and laced her fingers into the thick strands of his hair, arching her hips high so that he would know she was ready, so that he would feel how she ached for the moment of consummation.

He cupped his hands beneath her, holding her tightly against him. "You're beautiful, Lynn," he whispered, and his words carried her into the center of a vast universe, pulsating with the starbursts of her own desire.

And when the universe finally exploded into darkness, Adam was there, sharing her passion, waiting to take her down to the light on the other side.

CHAPTER NINE

SOME TIME DURING the night Adam converted the narrow sofa into a comfortable, queen-size bed. Lynn had a vague memory of standing and watching him, her own limbs too weighted and lethargic to move.

She remembered nothing more until she opened her eyes and discovered him pulling the coffee table close to the bed. Two trays, each containing a glass of orange juice and a plate of scrambled eggs and toast, rested on the center of the table.

She sat up in bed and propped herself against some pillows, but the soft, teasing words that sprang to her lips died unspoken when she looked more closely at Adam. The tension emanating from him was strong enough to create an almost visible aura. Suddenly self-conscious, she tucked the sheet over her naked breasts, clamping it against her sides with her elbows.

"Good morning," Adam said, staring out of the

window. She couldn't imagine what he found so interesting in the view of her neighborhood's rooftops. Without meeting her eyes he handed her one of the trays. "I thought you'd be hungry since we never got to eat dinner last night."

"Mmm, you're right. I'm starving. This looks delicious, Adam. I'm impressed. It's a long time since you cooked me a meal."

For a moment the level of tension in the room dropped as they both sipped orange juice. "Face it, Lynn," he said, grinning engagingly, "my cooking's been better than yours for the past sixteen years. You're never going to catch up with me, however many lessons your mother's been giving you recently."

"I think there's more than a hint of reverse chauvinism hidden in that remark," she said with deliberate lightness. "If I weren't still half-asleep, I'd call you on it."

He laughed, then his smile faded, and the tension immediately returned in full force. He pulled up a chair so that he could eat without sitting on the bed and began to munch on a piece of toast with dogged determination. He was wearing his slacks, which looked a bit crumpled after their night on the floor, but he was barefoot and he hadn't put on a shirt. Looking at him, Lynn could almost feel the springy resilience of the hair on his chest and the powerful ripple of his body muscles. Heat crept up into her cheeks, and she grabbed her glass, drinking the rest of her orange juice in a single swallow. The ice cold liquid had zero effect on her climbing temperature.

"I had to use the last four eggs," Adam said, breaking the strained silence. "There were ants crawling in the stuff you left out on the counter. I put it all down the drain, the leftover wine, too.

"That sounds like a wise move."

"My cleaning lady tells me there's been a plague of ants this past summer."

"I haven't noticed." Lynn chewed a small mouthful of scrambled eggs and toast, chiefly for something to do. She had never thought about what she and Adam might discuss the morning after a night of passionate lovemaking. Ants, however, seemed less than appropriate. She put down her fork.

"Adam, about last night . . . I didn't mean—"

"There's no need to explain," he said quickly. "Lynn, I understand what happened. Heaven knows, after all these years of feminist lectures from you, I realize that women have biological urges just like men do. As far as I'm concerned, the most important thing about last night is that we shouldn't allow what happened to mess up our real relationship. Your . . . friendship is very important to me, Lynn."

"I'm not quite sure what you're implying," she said quietly. "I told you last night that I wanted to make love to *you*, and I specifically said I wasn't just suffering from a sudden attack of jangling hormones. Did you think I was lying?"

"No! No, of course not. At least not intentionally." He pushed away his plate, abandoning the pretense of eating. "But last night was the culmination of a long and frustrating week for both of us. We probably felt and said things in the heat of the moment . . . Anyway, I want you to know that what happened yesterday needn't have any effect on our relationship. We've been friends for a long time— and making love to you—going to bed with you— oh, hell! I'm trying to explain that I understand that we both said things last night that it would be better for us to forget."

"You're beginning to babble as badly as a Comptex vice president, Adam. In plain English, are you saying that you don't mind if I asked you to make love to me because I felt in the mood to have sex with somebody and you happened to be available? You don't even mind if I lied when I said that I wanted you?"

For an instant she thought she saw pain reflected in his eyes, then his mouth tightened and the pain vanished as if it had never been. "I'm sorry if my explanations sound incoherent. I suppose I'm suffering from a guilty conscience and trying to apologize. That's never easy to do."

"You're apologizing for what happened between us last night?"

He didn't reply at once, and she drew a series of circles on the crumpled bedclothes with her fingernail. "I'd like an honest answer, Adam. Are you sorry you made love to me?"

His body became very still, and the room suddenly seemed very quiet. "No," he said finally. "No, I'm not sorry we made love, even though it makes life more complicated for both of us right now. And I'm not really apologizing for last night. What happened last night between us . . . well, I guess I'm apologizing for disturbing you and Damion on Thursday. I came at an inappropriate time and insisted that you let me into your apartment. I know I interrupted something important, and I suspect I didn't improve matters by pretending that you and I were planning to marry. I knew at the time that I was carrying our charade too far."

She said nothing, and he got up and walked to the window, keeping his back turned partly toward her when he spoke. "Relationships are fragile when they're just starting out, and once I'd interrupted you and Damion on Thursday night, I can guess that things may not have progressed the way you wanted when you saw him on Friday. I'm not an insensitive person, Lynn. In fact I would say I'm pretty sensitive to your moods. By the time you met me yesterday afternoon for our drive to Princeton, I knew something had made you nervous and ill at ease with me. You were on edge from the moment I picked you up."

"Meeting those Comptex vice presidents would be enough to make a bowl of Jell-O stand on edge."

He smiled, but his amusement faded quickly. "The Comptex executives, horrible as they were, can't be responsible for the fact that you carefully avoided talking about Damion. You never once mentioned him yesterday, at least not until I brought up the subject. I'm guessing that my intervention on Thursday night screwed things up pretty badly."

"It's true that I didn't talk about Damion. But it wasn't because I was too upset about him to mention his name."

"We don't have to pretend with each other, Lynn," Adam said gently. "It's been scarcely a week since you told me how much Damion means to you, and I know from personal experience how frustrating it is to love somebody who doesn't return your feelings."

"I can't think how." She tried to make a joke of the situation. "According to my mother you've never even looked at a woman who wasn't immediately bowled over by your devastating charm."

His smile didn't reach his eyes. "I've told you already this week that parents can be unreliable sources of information."

Suddenly pain ripped through her at the thought of Adam loving another woman. "You told me last weekend when we started this whole crazy charade . . . when you kissed me . . . that you were thinking about a woman you loved and transferring your feelings for her to help you act out a role with me. Doesn't that woman return your feelings?" She forced her mouth into a reasonable facsimile of a smile. "Mom will never believe that story."

"I'm not sure this is the right moment to talk about it, Lynn. We've had enough misunderstandings between us over the past few days. Let's not add to them. Look, we've always teased each other about modern woman's role in a changing world, and we've argued at least a zillion times about the differences between the emotional and physical needs of the two sexes. But if we put all the teasing aside and speak honestly, we both know sexual frustration is a force to be reckoned with, and of course, I accept that women can suffer from it as much as men. In retrospect I can see exactly how things got out of hand between us last night. It's my fault. I should have never agreed to come up to your apartment."

"I think your nobility is a touch out of place, Adam. I don't remember resisting much when you seduced me."

He shrugged. "Maybe not. Maybe that's not a relevant comment."

Lynn resisted the urge to scream with frustration. He seemed to be absolutely determined to gloss over the magic of everything that had happened between them and pretend it had just been a run-of-the-mill sexual dalliance. She twisted around on the bed to see him more clearly and noticed the tension in the rigid lines of his back. If he hadn't indicated that he was suffering from a bad case of unrequited love, she would have told him straight out that she loved him. But in the circumstances such a confession seemed inappropriate, even though she felt confident that he desired her sexually a great deal more than he was willing to admit.

If he desired her physically and also liked her as a friend, could love be far away? She didn't know. As she had recently learned, love was an elusive emotion that could sometimes be hard to recognize, and she wasn't sure that in Adam's case warm friendship and sexual attraction necessarily added up to true love. Was it fair to burden him with her feelings? Did she have any right after her recent behavior to tell him that she loved him?

"You seem to have my motivations wonderfully well analyzed, Adam," she said, covering her uncertainty with a veil of sarcasm. "How about yours? It's fascinating to learn that I was simply using your body to sublimate my uncontrollable urges for another man, but I'm curious to know why you were such a willing partner. Did you take me to bed out of straightforward male sexual aggression? Or did you consider it a case of turnabout being fair play? Maybe I was nothing more to you than a convenient substitute lover. When you made love to me, were you imagining I was somebody else?"

He must have seen the spark of anger in her eyes, or perhaps she hadn't controlled the tremor of hurt in her voice as well as she had hoped. He lifted his hand toward her in a curiously comforting gesture, then allowed it to drop back to his side. "Of course I wasn't imagining you were somebody else," he said tersely. "How could you ever think I would be so insulting to you?"

"Easily, because I'm merely reversing our positions. You've already informed me that I was imagining you were Damion Tanner. Why is it insulting for me to make a similar suggestion about you?"

He winced. "I have the impression that the more we try to explain, the deeper we're wading into the mire. Lynn, you're not a nameless sex object to me; you're a very dear friend."

"I'm not sure I want to be your very dear friend, Adam."

He spoke quickly. "Look, don't say anything more. Trust me, Lynn. This isn't the right moment for either of us to make major decisions about anything personal. We probably shouldn't waste our time analyzing what happened last night. We've been friends for too many years to let a single mistake have a permanent effect on our relationship. What matters now is the future, not what happened yesterday. You have my word that you won't have to fend off my unwanted sexual advances. I can assure you that what happened last night won't be repeated."

She was shaken by the intensity of the anger that surged through her. "Are you absolutely certain of that?" she asked, wondering if he could hear the ominous lack of emphasis in her voice. "You're not planning to make love to me ever again?"

He swung around from his inspection of the rooftops, the hint of mockery in his expression readily apparent. "Yes, I'm absolutely certain. I promise I'm not going to be driven crazy by the sight of your luscious body. I'm not going to succumb to a frenzied urge to throw you onto a bed and make love to you every time we happen to meet. Our relationship has much more to it than trivial sexual attraction."

"Oh." Lynn smiled tightly, her brain racing feverishly. "Well, that's reassuring news, Adam. Its certainly good to know that last night was nothing more than a one-time fit of mental aberration on your part, and not something to be taken seriously. Heaven knows, it would be terribly annoying for me if you'd found my lovemaking so satisfying and so special that you longed to repeat the experience. It's a relief to know you find me so easily resistible. It's a good thing I'm not too experienced as a lover, or you might have become addicted."

He looked disconcerted at this interpretation of his remarks, but she yawned delicately, as if dismissing their discussion, then put her breakfast tray onto the floor.

"If you'll carry our trays into the kitchen, Adam, I'll clean up in a minute. You cooked the meal, so it's my turn to put things away. I just want the luxury of spending another few minutes in bed."

She leaned back against the pillows, resting her head on her cupped hands. At the precise moment that Adam bent down to pick up the tray, she allowed the sheet to slide down to her waist. Dark color stained his cheeks as he straightened up and found himself staring down at the pink and white nakedness of her breasts. He swallowed hard.

"I'll put these trays in the kitchen," he said hoarsely.

Lynn closed her eyes and wriggled languorously against the pillows. The sheet slipped another two inches down her body. "You do that, Adam," she said. "I'll just lie here a little longer. It's so comfortable."

It was at least five minutes before he emerged from the kitchen, and by then she had had plenty of time to still any uneasy prickings of her conscience. She kept her eyes closed, but the sheet was now tangled somewhere around her knees. She heard Adam gulp as he approached the end of the bed. She estimated that he halted at least five feet away.

"I'll take that shower now, Lynn," he said, his voice breaking huskily in the middle of her name.

She opened her eyes as if just becoming aware of

him and slowly sat up. The sheet gradually curled into
a heap around her ankles. She yawned again, stretched
luxuriously and heard him give another strangled gulp.
When she had finished stretching, she smiled, her
brown eyes glowing with limpid innocence.

"We could shower together if you like," she suggested breathlessly. "It would save time."

"No!" He ran one of his hands agitatedly through
his hair, then spoke again, more calmly. "No, of course
we couldn't shower together. Your shower is too small
for two people."

"But that makes it all the more fun," she murmured,
getting out of bed and walking toward him.

Seeing how much effort it was costing him not to
stare longingly at her naked body, she allowed herself
the luxury of a quick, inward sigh of relief. It was
good to see some confirmation of her suspicion that
Adam had found their lovemaking as cataclysmic as
she had.

"Don't you think taking a shower together sounds
like fun?" she whispered, trailing her fingers down
the side of his face, then continuing down his bare
chest to the belt of his slacks.

His cheeks were no longer flushed, but deathly
pale. "What are you trying to do, Lynn?" he asked
curtly, but his pallor belied the brusqueness of his
words.

Her hand continued its downward progression. "I
don't think I'm trying to do anything," she murmured.
"I think I'm succeeding."

"Let me rephrase my question," he said, and his
voice suddenly seemed laced with deliberate cruelty.
"Precisely what are you hoping to prove by these
efforts to seduce me?"

"I'm hoping to prove that you're a fool," she said
softly.

His laughter was harsh. "Oh, I concede that point already, Lynn. I'm a Grade-A, number one fool. You can call off your test."

"I can't call it off yet," she murmured. "It's only been partially successful. Agreeing that you're behaving irrationally is just the first stage. Stage two requires you to take steps to correct the foolish behavior we identified in stage one."

His body was suddenly hard against her thighs, and his breath warm against her mouth. "Do you have any practical suggestions for stage two?" he asked huskily.

"Make love to me again," she whispered. "I need you to love me, Adam."

There was no longer any emotion in his voice but the anguish of suppressed desire. "Dammit, Lynn, you know that isn't a smart move for either of us."

"Hush." She put her mouth over his and felt his lips tremble briefly beneath hers before his arms came around her, crushing her to him. He kissed her until her body moved hungrily against his.

He didn't bother to carry her to the bed, and she couldn't possibly have walked there. They collapsed together onto the floor. The thick carpet felt smooth against her back; above her, the hair on his chest was wiry and tantalizing against her breasts.

His kiss deepened, and a fine mist dewed her skin. Her breath shortened to a series of shallow gasps as his knowing fingers caressed her. She twisted against his thighs as he removed his slacks, and they sighed in mutual pleasure when her skin finally brushed unimpeded against his.

She had thought that, after the previous night, she could not achieve any greater fulfillment, but he led her to a point where body and soul seemed to mingle with a new, almost frightening completeness. And when she knew that she couldn't bear another moment's delay in their ultimate union, Adam took her over the brink, smothering the soft, shuddering cries of her climax with the ardor of his own devastating release.

Afterward, when they could both move again, he picked her up and laid her on the bed. "I'm going to take a shower," he said, and walked quickly into the bathroom before she could speak.

Easing off the bed, she slipped into her terry-cloth robe and cleared up the kitchen, although Adam hadn't left much mess. She straightened the covers on the bed and returned it to its daytime position, then surveyed the impersonal tidiness of her living room. Strange, she thought, how easy it was to wipe away all trace of events from inanimate objects and how impossible it was to erase the memory of what had happened from her body and soul.

"The bathroom's all yours," Adam said, returning fully clothed to the living room. Despite the fact that his shirt and jacket had been soaked the night before and that his pants had spent several hours on the floor, he looked neat, self-possessed, and alarmingly in control. His emotions, Lynn decided, must shed wrinkles as easily as his clothes.

"Thank you," she said stiltedly, finding it even more difficult to talk to him now than first thing that morning. Her body felt stiff and awkward as she walked into the bathroom, and it was a relief to stand under the needle-sharp spray of the shower. Yet she couldn't regret her deliberate seduction, she reflected as she smoothed soap over her legs. Their lovemaking this morning proved beyond all possibilty of doubt that Adam desired her with an intensity that matched her own. Surely it shouldn't be impossible to convince him that a lifelong friendship, allied to an unusually strong sexual attraction, was a combination rare enough to treasure.

The phone started to ring just as she turned off the shower. She wrapped a towel around herself and hurried into the kitchen, holding out her hand to take the receiver from Adam.

"It's your father," he said, his voice sounding tight with strain as he handed her the phone.

"Hi, Dad!" she said cheerfully, propping herself against the wall as she talked. "It's good to hear from you."

"Hello, Lynn dear." Her father's dry, New England voice was mellowed by affection. "I'm glad to find you home. Your mother's busy at the reception desk, so she asked me to call and confirm that you'll be catching the early train today when you come up to visit. But since Adam's there, I suppose you're planning to drive up in his car. We're especially looking forward to seeing you because we have something important to discuss with you."

For a man about to face the expiration of an important contract deadline he sounded amazingly chipper and carefree. Lynn glanced at the clock built into the oven and saw that it was already eleven o'clock. The Comptex contract deadline expired at five that evening, and she was horrified to realize that, in the crush of everything else that had happened, she and Adam had almost forgotten about it. Now that she actually thought about it, she found it extraordinary that her parents hadn't called before now to find out her decision and to discuss their plans.

"You sure do have something to tell me!" she said. "I can't believe you waited this long to call. Good grief, Dad, it's only a few hours till the Comptex deadline expires!"

"The Comptex deadline?" he repeated. "What are

you talking about, Lynn?"

"It's no good to sound innocent and bewildered, Dad. That ploy won't work anymore. I'm twenty-six years old, which ought to be old enough for you and Mom to confide in me, even if you don't want me to feel pressured. Anyway all your tact and discretion were wasted in the end. Adam told me the whole story when he came to my apartment Thursday night. Surely you didn't expect him to keep your plans a secret. He understood that I had a right to be involved in the decision, even if you two stubborn people were determined to keep me out of it. How could you possibly think my career in Manhattan was so important that I wouldn't want to come home and help out in a crisis? I'm hurt that you and Mom didn't tell me what was going on."

She heard her father clear his throat. "Adam told you the whole story? Um . . . what exactly did he say, Lynn?"

"He told me about Comptex's offer and the deadline on selling the inn, of course. About you and Mom needing me to take over the job of manager and about you both being reluctant to tell me how much I was needed at home."

"Adam told you we were selling the inn to Comptex Corporation?"

"Dad, this is a crazy conversation. Why are you repeating everything I say?"

"Must be a first sign of creeping senility," he said dryly. "The fact is, Lynn, you're not making a whole lot of sense to me."

She became aware that Adam was still standing next to her, his fingers drumming restlessly on the kitchen counter. "Look, could you hold on a moment?" she asked her father. "Adam's right here, and I think he wants to say something."

She turned away from the receiver. "What is it, Adam? Do you want to tell me something?"

"I'd like to speak to your father, if I could," he said, and the quietness of his words did not quite disguise their urgency.

She regarded him curiously, intrigued when she saw a faint trace of embarrassment flare momentarily in his eyes.

"Sure. Of course you can talk to him." She spoke into the phone again. "Dad, I'll catch up with you later. I'm sure Adam will tell you not to do anything on that Comptex deal until we get up there. Say hi to Mom, and tell her we're looking forward to dinner. We're both starving."

She handed the phone to Adam, who gripped the receiver tightly. "Ted?" she heard him say as she walked to the closet to select some clothes. "Adam here. Lynn and I will be driving up to see you as soon as we get organized. I'll explain everything then."

She carried her clothes into the bathroom and shut the door, leaning against it thoughtfully. "There is something extremely strange going on here," she informed the mirror. "No wonder I've taken to speaking to my own reflection. These last few days it talks more sense that anybody else I know."

When she finished dressing and came out of the bathroom, Adam was waiting by the front door, obviously poised for a quick getaway.

"I have to go back to my apartment and get changed," he said hurriedly. "I'll be back here by twelve-thirty. Would you wait for me downstairs in the lobby?"

"Yes, of course. Adam, about that Comptex offer. Why did Dad sound so puzzled? Listening to him, I had the impression he'd never even heard about the deadline on their contract."

"We'll talk about it in the car," he said. "I don't have time to explain right now, not if we want to get to Connecticut by mid-afternoon. Good-bye, Lynn. I'll see you downstairs in a little while."

He almost ran out the door. She locked it thoughtfully behind him, then pulled her overnight case from the top shelf of the closet and began stuffing clean underclothes randomly inside it. She dropped a pinch of fish food into her aquarium, her brows wrinkling as she watched the glittering neons swim disdainfully past the colored flakes. From the moment she'd picked up the phone and spoken to her father, Adam had shown all the symptoms of a nervous man with a very guilty conscience. She wondered why.

Returning to the bathroom, she scooped her makeup into a cosmetics bag, then dumped it into the top of her case. It suddenly occurred to her that the most logical reason for Adam's guilty conscience was the fact that he had just seduced the only daughter of two of his oldest and dearest friends. His outdated male code of honor probably made it very uncomfortable for him to talk to a man whose unmarried daughter was standing close to his side, wet and naked except for a pink bath towel.

"Oh, *hell!*" she said, not at all pleased with her own rationalization. She didn't want Adam to feel guilty about their lovemaking. She wanted him to feel enraptured, entranced, bedazzled—all the emotions that she was feeling. She slammed the lid of her case shut with a violence that was totally alien to her nature, then drooped onto the sofa and stared disconsolately at the fish tank. As usual the angelfish were gobbling up all the food, which made her wonder how the neons and the tetras managed to survive. She wondered how she would manage to survive if Adam took off for California and resumed his affair with the mysterious woman who supposedly didn't love him. How could any woman be crazy enough not to love Adam, once he turned the full force of his potent charm in her direction?

The closet door was open, and she stared into the mirror attached to the inside of the door. She looked sultry-eyed, hollow-cheeked, and subtly wanton. Would her parents notice how much her appearance had changed in the past week? Would they notice that she trembled every time Adam came near her? Sighing, she shut the closet door, pushing an errant tangle of curls out of her eyes.

Falling in love with your best friend, she was beginning to realize, could cause more problems than she had ever dreamed of a week ago, in those seemingly far distant days when she had been too foolish to know the secrets of her own heart.

CHAPTER TEN

ONCE THEY HAD escaped the worst of the Manhattan traffic, Lynn decided the moment had come to insist on some specific answers to her long list of questions.

"I would really like to know what's going on with this Comptex offer," she told Adam. "Why didn't my father sound more concerned about the deadline? According to you, my decision was so crucial that you interrupted my date with Damion at midnight simply to find out how I would react to the idea. But on the phone just now my father sounded as though he'd never heard of a job offer to me, or a contract deadline, particularly one that's due to expire this afternoon."

"We seem to be rehashing an awful lot of old explanations," Adam said tightly. "I've apologized at least three times for coming around to your apartment and interrupting your date with Damion. It was a misjudgment on my part. I realize now that I should have phoned you on Friday morning at the office, and that way we'd never have gotten ourselves into such a difficult situation last night."

"Do you know, I think I resent your dismissing what happened last night as a *difficult situation*. That's not the way I see it."

His hands tightened on the steering wheel. "Before we talk any more about that, Lynn, I need some honest answers from you. Last weekend you told me you were in love with Damion Tanner. You admitted you very badly wanted him to take you to bed. On Tuesday evening and again on Thursday night I had the impression that he was more than willing to fulfill every one of your most exotic fantasies. Yet this morning when we woke up, you made love to me as if..." He ran his fingers impatiently through his hair. "I guess I'd just like to know exactly what the current situation is between you and Damion Tanner."

She drew in a long, deep breath. "Damion Tanner is my boss. He's an extraordinarily talented actor, and I admire his acting ability and his dedication to his career. When he's performing, or even when he's listening to a competent professional offering advice, he's an awesome sight. As you know, he's signed recently to do a feature movie. I think he's going to be the major male star of the next decade."

"So you'll be going with him to L.A. when he makes his movie?"

"No, I don't think so."

He looked up sharply. "Then you've reached a favorable decision about working at Wisteria Inn?"

"Adam, it took me about two minutes to realize that I would much prefer to manage a successful country inn than act as general gofer for a movie star, however talented he happens to be. You and my parents have all badly misunderstood me. I can't imagine why you all thought that asking me to move to Connecticut would present me with such a difficult set of choices."

"In career terms I thought you might consider the choice easy. But the personal decision would have to be difficult if you're in love with Damion Tanner."

"It didn't seem so to me," she said quietly. "Which probably tells us both something about my feelings for Damion. The fact is, Adam, that even if this whole issue of managing Wisteria Inn hadn't come up, I don't think things would ever have worked out between us. The only thing Damion and I have in common is a love of acting and the performing arts."

"Six and a half days ago you told me you were dying of a terminal case of unrequited love."

"Yes, well, last week I wasn't seeing things as clearly as I might have. In some ways you could call my feelings for Damion Tanner a final fling with adolescence. Suddenly I'm all grown up, even if it has taken me quite a while to make it. I'm sorry you've had such a trying week witnessing the process."

She looked out the window, although there wasn't much to see other than gray, overcast skies and speeding cars. They were nearing the exit ramp for her parents' inn. "How about you, Adam? I've bared my soul; now it's your turn. A couple of times recently you've mentioned a woman you're in love with who doesn't return your feelings. Are you still hoping that something will come of that relationship?"

He switched to the exit lane, then glanced briefly away from the road, his gaze searching as it rested on her face. "I think I am," he said. "In fact, I'm beginning to have quite high hopes that it will all work out much sooner than I'd dreamed. Once we get over another couple of rough spots that are all my own fault. She's an elusive quarry."

Lynn swallowed hard over the lump in her throat. "Who is she, Adam?"

There was a short pause. "I don't think this is the right moment to tell you, Lynn."

"Why not?" She forced herself to smile, although the effort nearly killed her. "We're old friends, Adam. I'd like to hear all about the woman who's finally captured that impregnable heart of yours. My mother will never believe it when she hears you've been conquered at last. I hope this woman, whoever she is, soon learns to reciprocate your feelings." She sat on her crossed fingers and hoped God would forgive her for the lie.

"I hope so, too." Adam suddenly grinned, his expression inexplicably self-satisfied. "You know, I've just decided I'll tell you all about her later on this evening. Right now we're only five minutes away from the inn, and my mind is pretty much on the Comptex deal and the need to talk things over with your parents." His smile widened. "When I tell you about the love of my life, I'd like to have time to do the subject justice. You can understand that, I'm sure. She's a very special woman, you know, and it's taken me quite a while to attract her attention. For a while there I was wondering if I'd have to hire a plane and a skywriter before she'd notice what I felt for her."

"It seems to me it's a pity she isn't a bit more observant," Lynn said tartly.

Adam looked amused. "Believe me, I've often felt that way myself."

Lynn sighed. "Well, I'm glad she's so special," she said, her voice as hollow as her emotions. "I'll look forward to meeting her." She curled into a small, tight ball in the corner of the seat and stared out the window, her misery so intense that she was scarcely aware of the familiar landmarks flashing by as Adam drove the last couple of miles to her parents' inn.

The chill in the air when they arrived was much more noticeable than it had been even a week earlier. The storm that had hit Manhattan the previous night had obviously hit Connecticut as well. The trees were not yet completely bare, but they had to walk through a layer of sodden brown leaves to reach the rear entrance to the inn, and Lynn was glad to feel a comforting wave of warmth envelope them as soon as they entered the short back hallway.

Her parents, who were sitting in the family room, jumped up eagerly, exclaiming with pleasure as they welcomed the new arrivals. They greeted Lynn with kisses and warm hugs and, as always, embraced Adam as enthusiastically as a son. The air smelled of a wonderful mixture of baking and wood smoke, and the three dogs, who had been dozing contentedly on the hearth rug, leaped up and added their hysterical yaps to the general welcome. The largest mutt, who weighed eighty-five pounds and looked vaguely like a golden retriever, put his paws on Lynn's shoulders and licked her face with complete disregard for her fashionable new makeup. The two smaller dogs barked in unison as they raced in and out of everybody's legs, collapsing periodically to pant in exhausted heaps in front of the fire.

The scene was so familiar and so welcoming that Lynn had no idea who was most astonished when, for absolutely no apparent reason, she suddenly burst into tears. The tears cascaded unchecked down her cheeks as she patted her pockets in a useless search for a handkerchief. Her mother, usually so efficient, was too surprised even to offer a tissue. The dogs stopped barking and tripping over their own tails, their mouths dropping open in a parody of human amazement, while

Adam watched her with an uncharacteristic appearance of helplessness. For several long minutes there wasn't a sound in the room other than the hiss of moisture escaping from the logs and the hiccupping of Lynn's sobs.

Adam was the first to move. Still looking uncomfortable, even a bit guilty, he silently thrust his handkerchief into her hand. She took it and blew her nose fiercely, but to her annoyance, the ridiculous tears continued to roll down her cheeks.

"Lynn, dear, what on earth is wrong?" her father asked. "Is there anything we can do to help? Please tell us."

She gulped back another sob. "Nothing's wrong," she said. "I don't know why I'm crying. Maybe I've developed a sudden allergy or something."

"It must be quite an allergy," her father remarked dryly. He watched in impotent sympathy as yet another tear dripped down her cheeks and fell into Adam's soggy handkerchief.

"I know what I'll do. I'll make some tea." Her mother sprang up with sudden decisiveness. Lynn's grandmother had been English, and Mrs. Frampton had inherited the belief that tea was the perfect answer to most of life's problems.

Lynn managed to produce a watery smile. "Please don't, Mom. I never have been able to convince you that I hate tea."

"I'm not making it for you to drink. I'm making it so that I can feel useful," her mother said, sighing with relief as Lynn's flood of tears gradually slowed to a trickle. "But since you've stopped crying, I suppose I can forgo the therapy."

"Why don't I pour us all a glass of sherry?" Mr. Frampton suggested. "I have dry or medium sweet, whichever you prefer."

Lynn agreed that sherry was an excellent idea and sat down on the sofa next to her mother while her father poured the drinks. Adam perched on the edge of an armchair drawn up close to the fire.

"Are you sure you don't want to talk to us about anything?" her father said, his voice quiet but wonderfully reassuring as he handed her a glass of sherry.

Her tears had stopped as swiftly and irrationally as they had come, and now she felt dry, even arid, as if she would never in her entire life shed another tear.

"There's nothing to tell," she said with determined cheerfulness. Sipping her drink, she forced herself to meet her parents' worried gazes. "Honestly, I've got no idea what brought on that dramatic display. I'm a bit angry with you both, but certainly not angry enough to develop hysterics the minute I cross over your threshold."

"Why are you angry with us?" her mother asked, her face and voice both indicating bewilderment.

"Because of this deal with Comptex, of course. I want to know why you both allowed the situation to get almost to the wire before telling me about it."

"Down to the wire?" Mr. and Mrs. Frampton exclaimed in unison.

"Yes." Lynn didn't attempt to conceal a touch of impatience. One way and another it had been a rough week—a cataclysmic week—and she was a bit tired of everybody's evasions. "If Adam hadn't told me about the offer you got from Comptex Corporation, I don't think you'd have told me you were planning to sell the inn until after the deal was complete."

"The deal was complete?" Her father seemed to realize that he was once again parroting everything she said. "Oh...uh...well, you should never have worried about...uh...that," he added uncomfortably.

His stumbling response was entirely out of character, and some instinct made her glance over her shoulder—just in time to catch Adam making frantic hand signals in her father's direction.

She stood up, drawing herself to her full five feet five inches. "Adam, I want to know what's going on here," she said.

"Nothing's going on," her father interjected hurriedly. "Your mother and I are thinking of retiring, that's all, and we mentioned that fact to Adam. We should have told you earlier, but we didn't want you getting worried over something that was still so vague and quite possibly months in the future."

Her voice was brittle with anxiety. "I want the truth, Dad. Is there any reason for me to worry? Adam says you're both every bit as healthy as you look. Is that true?"

"Dear, both of us are in excellent health," her mother said. "I can assure you that we both have normal blood pressure, sound hearts, and I've even got all my own teeth. We're not ready for the geriatric ward just yet."

"Then why all this secrecy about a simple business decision?"

"It's only natural for us to think about our retirement," her father said so heartily that she almost didn't notice his evasion. "I'll be sixty-eight next birthday, and your mother isn't exactly a spring chicken any more. We've worked in the same place for thirty-five years, and sensible people know that they ought to quit while they're still ahead of the game."

Adam sprang to his feet. "Well, I have to go and let my father know we've arrived," he said. "Would you care to walk across to his cottage with me, Ted? I feel in the mood for some exercise, and I'd appreciate your company."

"Wonderful idea. I could do with a brisk walk

myself." Both men avoided mentioning the lowering
skies which were visible outside the sitting room window and the blustery wind which was howling threat-
eningly in the chimney stack.

"I'll come with you," Lynn said. "I'd like to say
hello to Adam's father."

"Oh, no! You don't want to go!" Her parents and
Adam all spoke with a single voice.

"You can see Adam's father at dinner tonight,"
Mr. Frampton said, trying to justify his refusal. "He
often takes a nap in the afternoon around this time,
and you wouldn't want to disturb him."

"Besides, I'd like you to give me your opinion on
some new apricot jam we've just opened," her mother
interjected hurriedly. "I followed a different recipe,
and I'm afraid it's turned out too sweet. And I want
to show you the new microwave ovens we had in-
stalled. Your father and I are very pleased with them,
and the cook's absolutely thrilled. They actually work
quite efficiently."

"I'm really not into ovens, Mom. Not even micro-
waves."

"Lynn, I'm sorry, but there are a couple of things
I have to discuss privately with Adam," her father
said. "We'd like to take this walk alone."

"At least you're finally being honest," she muttered. "Sure, go ahead and take your walk and talk
to each other about Comptex. Lord knows it's only
right that the womenfolk should keep out of the way
in the kitchen while you men organize the important
business affairs of the family. Who knows what havoc
we might wreak if we were allowed to give our opinions on whether you should sign that contract or not."

"Nobody's planning to sign any contracts with
Comptex," her mother said decisively. "You can put
all worries about that right out of your mind. I'm sure

Adam and your father will explain everything to you later."

Ignoring Lynn's state of simmering temper, she smiled at her companionably as they walked toward the kitchen. "Let's try out that jam on some hot biscuits. You're looking too thin, you know. I don't think you ever eat when you're in the city."

Lynn followed her mother into the kitchen, then retreated to a distant corner of the room when the cook barely managed to conceal her displeasure at the invasion of two extra bodies into her domain when she was rushing to complete preparations for dinner.

"All right, Mom," Lynn said wearily. "You can cut out the act about the jam and the microwave ovens. Why didn't you want me to go with Dad and Adam?"

"No special reason," her mother said, disappearing into a huge walk-in pantry. "I just thought you might want to go up to your room and freshen up a bit. You have purple and black streaks on your cheeks from crying."

Her voice became muffled, presumably as she progressed further into the storage cupboard. "That's not a way to attract a man's attention, not even these days. I may be sixty-four years old and forty years out of date on courting rituals, but there's still nothing like a fresh complexion to make a man sit up and take notice."

"When you start talking about your age, I know you're desperate to change the subject. Whose attention am I supposed to be trying to attract? The busboy's? The bartender's? The busboy is already in love with all three chambermaids, and the bartender is about to celebrate his sixtieth birthday. As far as I know, those are the only two men around this inn other than Dad."

Her mother returned with a small pot of apricot

jam. "You've forgotten the gardener," she said, smiling sweetly and holding the jar up to the light. "Here, I found it at last. I'll pop a couple of biscuits onto a plate, and you can take them up to your room with a cup of fresh coffee. That's one of the nice things about running a hotel restaurant; we always have coffee ready-brewed."

She walked over to the bank of automatic drip coffee makers and almost without pausing for breath added, "Adam is extraordinarily good-looking, and of course he's very successful in his career. Not to mention how successful he is with women. But I wouldn't let that intimidate me, if I were you, Lynn. After all, he's had ample opportunity to marry over the past ten years, and he never has."

Lynn spoke through tightly clenched teeth. "What has Adam got to do with this conversation, Mother?"

"I've no idea, Lynn dear. I was hoping you could tell me. Do you think he would like some hot biscuits and jam, too? When he gets back from seeing his father, of course."

"I don't know, Mom. I don't think I know anything at all about Adam's likes and dislikes, and I'm beginning to know less as each day goes by." She took the coffee from her mother and walked determinedly toward the kitchen door. "When you and Dad feel ready to tell me what's going on with this Comptex deal, I'll be in my room. For what it's worth, if you really do want me to take over the day-to-day management of Wisteria Inn, I'd be honored and flattered to try to cope with the job."

Her mother reached out and put her hand on Lynn's arm. "That's wonderful news, dear. Your father and I have been so very happy here; we always hoped you'd want to take over and build on the reputation we've managed to establish. I'm sure Dad will explain more fully later on, but I know he and Adam are hoping to thrash out some sort of a purchase agreement for the inn this weekend. They'll both be delighted to know that the problem of finding a manager is solved."

"Adam is planning to buy the inn?" If her mother had told her Genghis Khan had put in a bid, she couldn't have been more astonished. Although after the events of the past week, she thought, there ought to be nothing left that could actually surprise her. "Is he going to match the Comptex offer?"

"I'm not sure what the exact terms of the deal are going to be. You know me, I always leave the financial and administrative arrangements to your father. I'm more comfortable coping with the kitchen and the domestic matters."

Lynn smiled, the remnants of her temper disappearing in a wave of affection. "What I actually know is that my father has never made an important decision in his life without consulting you first, so you can cut out the powerless little woman act. It doesn't work with me."

Her mother laughed. "It works wonders with men of all ages, however. Personally I think it's a terrible shame that honesty between the sexes is so depressingly in fashion these days. It was much more fun when we could flutter our eyelashes and look helpless and a little bit mysterious. There's no evidence that the human race is any happier just because everybody nowadays feels compelled to spill their innermost emotional secrets within two minutes of making a new acquaintance."

There was a definite irony in her mother's remarks, Lynn thought as she sat down next to her bedroom window and sipped gratefully at the steaming cup of coffee. She and Adam could hardly be accused of indulging in instant intimacy. Sixteen years from first meeting to first bedding had to be a record in the modern world. The very warmth and depth of their friendship made it difficult to commit the ultimate intimacy of revealing the truth about their sexual emotions. Even at the height of their passion she had been afraid to tell Adam that she loved him. Yet Adam had shared more of her secret thoughts and dreams than any other person.

She bit into a jam-covered biscuit and paced nervously around her bedroom. Maybe Adam suffered from the same inhibitions she was suffering from. He had claimed to be in love with some unnamed woman, but was he actually telling the truth? Might he not be exaggerating his feelings for some casual girl friend in order to hide his feelings for Lynn? It was difficult to imagine Adam—cool, self-assured Adam—being reluctant to admit how he felt, but she supposed it was possible.

The delicious biscuits fired her body with new energy. She was just drying her hands after washing them when a knock came at her door. She hurried out of the bathroom, tossing the hand towel on the bed.

"Who is it?" she called.

"It's me, Adam. I'd like to come in and talk to you if I may."

"If it's anything about Comptex, I don't want to hear it."

"It's not about Comptex," he said. "I want to tell you all about the woman I'm in love with."

She opened the door a crack. "It's been a tough week, Adam, and I'm feeling fresh out of generosity and nobility of spirit right now. I'm not sure I want to hear about her."

"I think you should. It's taken me about sixteen years to work up the courage to tell her that I love her. Don't you what to be around to hear me make an ass out of myself if I do it wrong?"

Hope leaped up and wedged itself as a solid lump in her throat. She swallowed hard. "Maybe you'd better come in," she said. "After sixteen years, I guess you deserve a hearing."

He walked in and locked the door behind him. Light from the window struck the planes of his face, highlighting the aquiline cast of his features and the thickness of his blond hair. He looked almost indecently attractive. If Greek gods ever had tans, Lynn thought, they must have looked like Adam.

She lowered her gaze, afraid it might be too revealing. "Do you want to sit down?" she asked.

"No, not right now, thanks. I think I can tackle this better standing up." He walked over to the small fireplace and leaned against the wooden mantel. "Where shall I start?" he said. "Do you want to hear about when I first realized I was in love with her?"

"Yes, please. I think I do."

A familiar mockery shone in his face when he turned to look at her, but she recognized now that his derision was directed entirely toward himself.

"It was graduation eve, and the love of my life got herself all dressed up for the high-school prom," he said. "She came floating into her parents' living room on the arm of her handsome, eighteen-year-old escort. She was dressed in white organdy—what else?—and he was wearing a tuxedo that didn't quite fit across the shoulders. He was captain of the football team, and he had muscles to prove it. Bubbling with excitement, she danced across the room to give her parents a kiss, and then she gave me one, too. The damn football captain didn't even blink. It didn't occur to him to be jealous of somebody who was obviously a member of an entirely different generation. He shook hands with her parents and then with me. He was a polite young man; he actually called me sir. When I shook his hand, I found myself fighting an overwhelming urge to ram his orthodontically perfect teeth straight down his handsome throat. It took me about two minutes to realize that I was madly in love with a not-quite eighteen-year-old girl, and ten seconds flat to decide that, since I was already nearly twenty-seven, there wasn't a thing in the world I could do about it except to fall out of love fast."

"And did you? Fall out of love fast, I mean."

"Not as fast as I should have.The young girl in question didn't help. The summer before she went to college, I think she decided that she was a little bit in love with me. Or maybe she just wanted to test her sexual wings in what seemed to her to be relatively safe waters. I don't think she realized what she did to my self-control for three long, hot months. She invented a hundred different excuses for us to be alone, and then, when we were lying on some deserted river bank, or when everybody else had gone to bed and we were strolling around the garden, she'd start flirting with me. Inexpertly, of course, and with the sort of naive wonder that simply made it all the more entrancing to a jaded twenty-seven-year-old who'd begun to pride himself on his sophistication."

Lynn's eyes opened wide at the sudden flood of memories from that half-forgotten summer. "I was so angry with you that vacation! You always seemed to be laughing at me."

"If you'd only known what I was really feeling!" He grimaced ruefully, then seemed to stare into the distance. "Her parents guessed what was going on, of course."

Lynn gulped in astonishment. "They did?"

"Oh, yes, parents usually do, you know. And that was when this girl's mother took me to one side and pointed out that her daughter needed time to grow up before she started falling in love with somebody she'd hero-worshipped since fifth grade."

"What did you do when you were warned off?"

"My career was becoming more demanding at that stage, and I was beginning to travel a lot. I decided to branch out on my own and concentrate on my career for a while." He grinned. "Then, before too long, I made the wonderful discovery that the world was full of attractive women who were eager to help me find a cure for my problem."

"I'll bet you found the cure so pleasant that you soon forgot what the disease was," she said tartly.

"Not quite." His grin flashed briefly again. "Although I admit that mending my broken heart wasn't all pain and anguish."

"But it did mend," she said, a hint of a question in her voice.

"Yes, but it didn't seem to grow together into quite the same shape. I was a great deal less romantic and susceptible, although I still found lots of women attractive, of course."

"Of course."

He smiled at her irony and cast her a quizzical, loving glance that made her pulse race and her heart thump wildly against her rib cage. "The truth is, I even enjoyed a couple of fairly long-term relationships with women who deserved much more than I was able to give them. The trouble was that when it got right down to the nitty-gritty, when it got down to the moment when I had to decide if this was the woman I wanted to share the rest of my life with, I could never manage to convince myself I'd found the right one."

"If you were waiting for your seventeen-year-old to grow up, you seem to have waited an awfully long time," Lynn said. "There are a lot of years between almost eighteen and twenty-six."

"I wasn't consciously waiting for her," he said. "The summer after she left high school I could easily have convinced her that she loved me enough to marry me. She was all too willing to be persuaded. For a while I wondered what would have happened if I'd gone ahead and married her and given her time to grow up afterward. Fortunately some vestige of sanity prevented me from making that particular mistake, and I soon realized that a marriage between us at that point in our lives would have been catastrophic. By the time she graduated from college I didn't think I had a hope in hell of persuading her to marry me."

"I think you were wrong," Lynn said softly. "I think you could have persuaded her to marry you any time you wanted to. She just didn't realize it."

He looked startled. "It certainly didn't seem that way from my perspective. She had a wonderfully full and successful life, and she made it plain in dozens of ways that friendship was all she wanted from good old reliable Adam. She always chose handsome young boyfriends who were connected with the entertainment industry, and she took great pleasure in parading them under my nose, ostensibly for my approval. She invariably introduced me as her old friend Adam, with a definite emphasis on the word *old*." His gaze rested for a moment on her flushed cheeks. "And I think she quite deliberately let me know when she parted with her virginity."

Lynn twisted her hands in her lap. "Looking back on it, I suspect maybe she wanted to make you jealous."

His expression was wry. "Lynn, my dearest love, if that was her aim, I can't begin to tell you how successful she was!"

"And so you drowned your sorrows in a succession

of affairs with some of the country's most gorgeous women. What a sacrifice!"

He grinned. "I wouldn't *exactly* describe it in those terms," he admitted. She picked up a pillow and threw it in his direction. "Don't you want to hear what happened next?" he asked, catching the pillow. "We're just getting to the most interesting part of the story."

"I can't imagine how you can find anything about this woman interesting," Lynn said. "She seems an incredibly imperceptive sort of person to me. I can't think why you put up with her for so long."

"I was addicted, I guess, and everybody knows that addicts behave in inexplicable ways. Are you recommending that I go cold turkey and never see her again?"

She scowled with mock ferociousness. "Tell me the end of the story. Please, Adam."

"While I was out in California I blew yet another chance to establish a worthwhile relationship, and I finally admitted to myself that it was time to get this woman out of my system one way or the other. I flew back to New York, determined to approach her honestly and suggest that maybe she might like to consider putting our friendship onto a different basis."

"But you didn't say anything to her," Lynn protested. "Not a word!"

"No, naturally not, because she didn't give me the chance to tell her anything. We spent the weekend at her parents' inn, just as we'd done a hundred times before, and all during dinner, I was plucking up my courage to tell her what was on my mind. After dinner she seemed anxious to get me alone, and my hopes began to skyrocket. Maybe she'd already begun to reach some of the same conclusions I'd reached. Maybe I was in for a pleasant surprise. I poured myself a large Scotch and tried to work out exactly what words I'd use to explain things to her. I was just drawing breath to confess how I felt about her when she dropped a bombshell right at my feet."

"The crazy woman told you she was in love with Damion Tanner," Lynn whispered.

Adam nodded. "But you haven't heard the worst of it yet. She followed up her announcement with a request for *my* help in getting Damion Tanner into *her* bed! I didn't know whether to laugh or cry. As I recall I did neither, merely helped myself to a second, large serving of whiskey."

"She was a fool," Lynn said flatly. "Dense about other people's feelings and blind about her own."

"I'm not sure it's accurate to describe the woman I love as a fool. Marginally half-witted, perhaps, and definitely a trifle slow on the uptake..."

She threw the other pillow at him, missing for the second time.

"Once my brain started functioning again," Adam went on, "I began to think that perhaps she was making a mistake. I had a gut feeling that she wasn't as much in love with Damion Tanner as she thought she was. And then I kissed her—really kissed her for the first time in our lives—and that was the final straw as far as I was concerned. I decided to heck with ethics and rules of fair play. I wasn't going to give her up to Damion Tanner without a struggle."

"Just because she was good at kissing?"

"Because I knew she couldn't possibly kiss me like that and be genuinely in love with another man."

"You were very sure of yourself."

"On the contrary, I was in a constant state of panic. But every time I kissed her, I felt a little bit more sure of my ground."

"But when she finally seduced you, you refused to admit that what had happened had any particular significance. Why, Adam?"

"Because I love you so much I'm out of my mind with it," he said, his mask of wry humor dropping away to reveal the fierce intensity of his emotions. "And because my guilty conscience was bothering me."

"Your guilty conscience about what? The fact that you weren't entirely honest when you offered to help me attract Damion's attention?"

"Partly that. When it was too late I began to wonder if I'd had any right to interfere in your relationship with Damion. Then there was the whole wretched business with Comptex." He sighed. "I suppose I'm going to have to come clean about this whole ridiculous Comptex thing."

"It would be nice," she said dryly.

"When you told me you were going out with Damion on Thursday evening, I was immediately convinced that I'd lost my gamble. I'd thrown you into his path, piqued his interest, aroused his jealousy, and now I was going to pay the price. It was obvious that he wanted you, and I couldn't think of a single reason why you wouldn't end up in his bed. I spent most of the night calling first your apartment and then his, trying to reassure myself that I was misjudging the situation, that you weren't about to become Damion's lover. When I dialed your number sometime after eleven and discovered that the phone had been taken off the hook, I think I went a little crazy. I tore around to your building and was pressing the intercom buzzer within ten minutes of discovering the phone wasn't working. Then, when you answered the intercom, I had to invent some legitimate reason for being there.

I've never thought so fast in my life."

"You mean that whole story about Comptex was a fabrication? But it couldn't have been, Adam. We went to their headquarters and discussed the sale with their vice presidents. They must have made an offer for Wisteria Inn."

"Yes, they did. And your parents had asked me to sound you out tactfully about the possibility of your taking on the job of manager. That part of my story was true. But the contract deadline is ten days away, Lynn, and your parents had already pretty much decided to reject it. They want to retire, but they're not in any mad rush, and they can afford to wait for the right buyer. I interrupted your date with Damion for no other reason than because I couldn't bear to imagine you in bed with him. I know I have no right to manipulate your decisions as much as I've been doing this past week. My only excuse is that I love you, and I needed you to love me in return."

"There was no possibility of me going to bed with Damion that night," she said softly. "Subconsciously I'd realized at least two days earlier that I was madly in love with you."

The sudden tensing of his body belied the casualness of his words. "Has the message percolated through to your *conscious* mind yet? Not that I want to rush you or anything."

She walked across to the fireplace and pressed her body close to his, her hands clasped lovingly around his neck. "Didn't you hear my heart thumping every time you came within two feet of me? It may take me a while to get there, but I can work out the state of my emotions all by myself if you give me a few years. Say sixteen or so. Of course I love you, Adam. I love you more deeply and more passionately than I thought

I would ever be capable of loving."

"So you don't resent the fact that I deliberately set out to break up your relationship with Damion?"

"When we're celebrating our golden wedding anniversary, I expect I'll still be reminding you how you coerced me into marriage against my will and against my better judgment," she said, smiling tenderly.

"This talk of golden weddings is very intriguing, but I don't seem to remember asking you to marry me."

"Try to stop me. If you haven't bought the license by next week, I'll tell Mom and Dad that you compromised my virtue and they'd better get out their shotguns."

"Have you ever noticed how even the most ardent feminist seems to revert to old-fashioned methods when the chips are down? Still, I suppose I'll have to make an honest woman out of you. I couldn't bear to disappoint your mother."

She made a fist and thudded it softly against his jaw. "Chauvinist!"

He caught her fist with one hand and, in a single swift movement, swept her into his arms, carrying her over to the bed. "I may as well live up to my evil reputation," he said. "Be silent, woman, while I make love to you."

"Can I tell you that I love you and then be silent?"

His eyes blazed silver with desire. "Yes," he said hoarsely. "I think I might allow that."

"I love you, Adam."

"And I love you, too. More than I know how to express."

"We have the rest of our lives to work on showing each other."

"That sounds wonderful," he muttered as he captured her other hand and held both of them against the pillow. "If you like, you can start showing me now."

He lowered his mouth to her throat and kissed the warm hollow at the base of her neck, running his hands over her body until she glowed with the heat of desire. When they were both naked, she drew his mouth slowly up to hers, breathing her love into their endless kiss. Their bodies flowed together, the union so complete that it was impossible to say who dominated and who submitted, who gave and who received until, in the end, they fell together in ecstasy.

The light had faded from the windows when Lynn finally turned and trailed a lazy hand over Adam's naked stomach.

He groaned, grasping her fingers and stilling their movement. "I hope that isn't a suggestion," he said.

She laughed. "Only that it's late and maybe we should go downstairs. We could call your father and invite him over for a celebratory dinner with my parents. I think they'll all be pleased, don't you?"

"They'll be ecstatic. I threatened to stop visiting my father if he told me once more how anxious he was to be a grandfather and what a wonderful mother you'd make for my children. He'd even started to mutter about promising genes. Then your mother caught me on the stairs as I was coming up here and told me there was a cancellation in the bookings for the private banquet room for a week next Saturday, and that she'd have no difficulty whatsoever in putting a wedding together with two weeks' notice."

"In case you didn't know it already, Mom's a powerful organizing force once she's set in motion. Are you prepared for a church ceremony with at least a hundred guests, miscellaneous cousins as flower girls, and the choir singing anthems as we parade down the aisle?"

"I've waited sixteen years," he said. "I'm ready for anything as long as I get you all to myself once it's over."

"We could barricade ourselves inside your apartment and take the phone off the hook."

"I was thinking more along the lines of a desert island, somewhere in the middle of the Pacific Ocean. We have a lot of loving to catch up on, you and I."

"But we have the rest of our lives to make up for lost time." She rested her head on his shoulder and sighed, a soft sigh of pleasure. "That sounds pretty good, doesn't it?"

His arms tightened around her, and his mouth brushed gently across her eyelids. "It sounds wonderful."

Second Chance at Love®

All of the above titles are $1.95
Prices may be slightly higher in Canada.

Available at your local bookstore or return this form to:

 SECOND CHANCE AT LOVE
Book Mailing Service
P.O. Box 690, Rockville Centre, NY 11571

Please send me the titles checked above. I enclose _____ Include 75¢ for postage and handling if one book is ordered; 25¢ per book for two or more not to exceed $1.75. California, Illinois, New York and Tennessee residents please add sales tax.

NAME_____

ADDRESS_____

CITY_____STATE/ZIP_____

(allow six weeks for delivery)   **SK-41b**

QUESTIONNAIRE

1. How do you rate _____

   (please print TITLE)

   ☐ excellent   ☐ good

   ☐ very good   ☐ fair   ☐ poor

2. How likely are you to purchase another book in this series?

   ☐ definitely would purchase
   ☐ probably would purchase
   ☐ probably would not purchase
   ☐ definitely would not purchase

3. How likely are you to purchase another book by this author?

   ☐ definitely would purchase
   ☐ probably would purchase
   ☐ probably would not purchase
   ☐ definitely would not purchase

4. How does this book compare to books in other contemporary romance lines?

   ☐ much better
   ☐ better
   ☐ about the same
   ☐ not as good
   ☐ definitely not as good

5. Why did you buy this book? (Check as many as apply)

   ☐ I have read other
      SECOND CHANCE AT LOVE romances
   ☐ friend's recommendation
   ☐ bookseller's recommendation
   ☐ art on the front cover
   ☐ description of the plot on the back cover
   ☐ book review I read
   ☐ other _____
      _____
      _____

(Continued...)

6. Please list your three favorite contemporary romance lines.

_____
_____
_____

7. Please list your favorite authors of contemporary romance lines.

_____
_____
_____
_____
_____
_____

8. How many SECOND CHANCE AT LOVE romances have you read? _____

9. How many series romances like SECOND CHANCE AT LOVE do you <u>read</u> each month? _____

10. How many series romances like SECOND CHANCE AT LOVE do you <u>buy</u> each month? _____

11. Mind telling your age?
       ☐ under 18
       ☐ 18 to 30
       ☐ 31 to 45
       ☐ over 45

☐ Please check if you'd like to receive our <u>free</u> SECOND CHANCE AT LOVE Newsletter.

We hope you'll share your other ideas about romances with us on an additional sheet and attach it securely to this questionnaire.

• •

Fill in your name and address below:
Name _____
Street Address _____
City _____ State _____ Zip _____

Please return this questionnaire to:
  SECOND CHANCE AT LOVE
  The Berkley Publishing Group
  200 Madison Avenue, New York, New York 10016